"McQuade uses natural imagery . . . and an infusion of strangeness and wonder that verges on the supernatural to connect these stories, which are also linked thematically. Piecing together these connections demands close reading—and rewards it, with details to savor. Short-story fans should be on the lookout for McQuade, whose style nestles somewhere between Elizabeth Strout's and Helen Oyeyemi's."
—*Booklist*

"As I read *Tell Me Who We Were*, I wanted to drown in its pages. I adored this remarkable, wonderful book of linked stories, held together by a mysterious death. The stories capture the longing of girlhood, the strangeness of motherhood, the pain and hopefulness felt in a marriage. Kate McQuade writes with beauty, grace, and an electric touch of magic."   —Annie Hartnett, author of *Rabbit Cake*

"[A]n art form in its own right, combining ancient cultural prototypes with modern settings written poetically. . . . This is a slim volume to ponder, full of writing to savor, to glean meaning from. It is the evocation of universal memory, imagination, and emotion—prose that is at once lyrical and deep, telling stories in a language and style that is uniquely McQuade's."
—Washington Independent Review of Books

"With exquisite imagery and lush prose, *Tell Me Who We Were* examines trauma, loss, and the inexplicability of time's passage through a series of linked stories that, despite heartbreak, reveal how deeply interconnected we all are. Kate McQuade is one of the most exciting writers I've read in years. I could read—and learn from—her prose all day and still want more, and the haunting, crackling-with-life world of this linked collection will long stay with me."
—Anne Valente, author of *Our Hearts Will Burn Us Down*

"Insightful, compassionate. . . . A truly wonderful collection."

—*Star Tribune* (Minneapolis)

"Kate McQuade's *Tell Me Who We Were* is the most refreshing work of contemporary literature I've read in years. The writing is dazzling, the characters are both dear and edgy (which makes them irresistible), and the author's courageous willingness to enter the most intimate human experience charges every page with brave news, pleasure, and illumination. The roots of this book are in ancient literature, but its spirit is stirringly twenty-first century. A virtuoso performance!"

—David Huddle, author of *The Story of a Million Years* and *The Faulkes Chronicles*

"The elegant, intimate stories in Kate McQuade's *Tell Me Who We Were* provide a revelatory glimpse into the dark magic of girlhood, the intense pulsations of young adulthood, and the fraught sensuality of womanhood. This is an artfully constructed, soulfully rendered collection whose characters, images, and questions will resonate long after you turn the last page."

—Keija Parssinen, author of *The Unraveling of Mercy Louis*

TELL ME WHO WE WERE

TELL ME WHO WE WERE

STORIES

KATE McQUADE

WILLIAM MORROW

An Imprint of HarperCollins*Publishers*

A hardover edition of this book was published in 2019 by William Morrow, an imprint of HarperCollins Publishers.

FIRST WILLIAM MORROW PAPERBACK EDITION PUBLISHED 2020.

Designed by William Ruoto

Library of Congress Cataloging-in-Publication Data has been applied for.

ISBN 978-0-06-286980-7

20 21 22 23 24 LSC 10 9 8 7 6 5 4 3 2 1

For Jimmy

someone will remember us
I say
even in another time

—Sappho fragment,
translated by Anne Carson

Contents

THE TRANSLATOR'S DAUGHTER   1

A MYTH OF SATELLITES   19

WEDGE OF SWANS   39

HELEN IN TEXARKANA   67

SING ME A SONG   103

TEN KINDS OF SALT   115

THERE WILL BE A STRANGER   149

IN THE HOLLOW   175

ACKNOWLEDGMENTS   191

The Translator's Daughter

―⁂―

WE WERE ALL a little bit in love with her.

Partly the good of her, and partly the bad. Partly the pretty, and partly the dark thing under the pretty. Brown eyes almost black, like coffee or chocolate. That's what it would feel like when she looked at you, like a taste. Sweet and bitter. She had that long blond hair like a spun-sugar tangle, the kind of hair we'd all crayoned ourselves into since kindergarten but didn't really have, the kind you wanted to reach out and touch, smooth down with your hand. The kind she could hide behind, face invisible at her desk in the back of the classroom, or the kind she could toss over her shoulder during morning break. All this light in it, all caught up in a web, the golden threads just like that fairy tale, thrown back with an authority that would have made us follow her anywhere.

Which is why we looked to Lilith when Mr. Arcilla died. Mr. Arcilla: we were in love with him too, but in a more immediate way. Handsome and scruffy and achingly tall, a little bit father and a little bit boy—that tangled magic of him, because that was our first year at

Briarfield, the year we were still figuring out what we wanted. He was just out of college, the first task of his short adulthood to teach twelve-year-old boarding school girls the fundamentals of Spanish or French, depending on the semester. Spanish or French, the languages of love, and that's what it felt like, watching him shape his mouth around the words we did not understand. The thick, dark rumble of his voice, as rough as whiskers or the hands of a man. How he tucked his shirts in and how they always crept themselves out, as if they didn't want to be constrained any more than we did. And his tongue rolling around the double *R* like a fiery little maraca. *Arriba*. Spanish then French, that was the plan. But he never made it to French because he got drunk one night and ended up at the bottom of Reed Pond, naked.

The general theory: a poorly angled dive on a hot day off the wrong dock after a dry Boston summer. Low water, poor perception. But the general theory, espoused by Headmistress Salk and the policemen who kept coming back to ask vague, sympathetic questions, left out the most important detail, the fact that we probed endlessly that fall, couldn't stop imagining, picking at, poking like a wound, shocking and repulsive yet tremendously appealing: *naked*. Of course, it meant a second swimmer. A secret love affair, a tryst in the woods, dirt along their bodies, leaves caught in his hair before that beautiful, final plunge . . . so many possibilities to linger over. (We liked to imagine this. Perhaps it was part of the strange, dreamy mind-set of that autumn of twelve years old, imagining things like this and wondering why we were imagining them. Perhaps this is why for many of us sex and death have always been, in our fantasies since then, weirdly intertwined.)

Mr. Arcilla. Our first real love, our first real loss. We felt it keenly then, as if he had left each one of us without a letter, without a goodbye, the whole tragic rejection of it heightened paradoxically by the fact that we all felt the same personal betrayal. Cast aside.

Disregarded. Left on our own, alone. The memory of him meaning more than he himself had ever meant to us—of course we can see that now. But then, the only thing we could feel was his loss, and the raw, pulsing mystery of the lover who had taken him away from us.

Was it any wonder we were determined to seek her out?

IT WAS LILITH who told us he'd be back. "The dead always come back," she said, "if they have something to say. All he needs is a translator."

We asked her what she meant. She had a way, sometimes, of speaking with both conviction and vagueness, which made us believe what she said even if we didn't understand it.

"You know. Someone who can hear him. Someone who can bridge the world of the dead with the world of the living." She sighed this slow, exasperated sigh, flicking her cigarette thoughtfully. She was a first-former, same as all of us—what they called seventh grade in normal schools back home—but still, she made us feel young. "I suppose I can sense it because I'm used to it. Since my dad was a trans-lator. And since he's dead and all."

"That's not what you told us before, Lilith. You told us your dad took off. That he left you and your mom." That was Evie, or at least that's the way we remember it—tall, slinky Evie with her bitten-down nails, watchful and shrewd behind long red bangs. Evie was a stick-ler for backstory coherence, a close attention to detail that probably came from her own history as a compulsive liar. But the truth is, any one of us could have objected. We respected Lilith, but we respected consistency more. It was necessary, given that we didn't have much else to count on.

"Death *is* a kind of taking off," said Lilith calmly. "A temporary one."

"Well, your dad's not a translator," said Romy, her voice glintier than usual. She crossed her arms and scrunched her brow, all pixie-cut punk and huff. "Let's be clear. He's just a *professor*."

Which was maybe a subtle distinction. But it was a vital one, sacred, our tenuous connection to Lilith and to each other: we were all the children of professors. The Seven Sisters, we called ourselves. Actually, there were only six of us, but no one else seemed to notice, and Seven Sisters sounded better—like a secret society, the Pleiades, the blue-blooded women's colleges, scholarly things we knew about and flashed like designer labels. We had learned quickly in the red-brick, old-tome world of Briarfield that professor parents were a commodity, a sign of good breeding. Not exactly a yacht, but something. And if other forms of wealth were closed to us (we were all poor by boarding school standards), then at least our parents had given us this: the bloodline of academia to mark us as elite.

But Lilith just shrugged, unfazed, cigarette hand as steady as stone. Not shaky like we would have been, always were, if challenged about life back home. "A person can be more than one thing at the same time. My dad, for instance, was a scholar of several disciplines. And he wouldn't have left me and Mom. For a while, the counselors tried to make me believe that, but it's not true. He told me so himself." She paused, searching our eyes. "He tells me all the time."

"Um, Lilith?" said Claire politely. "You just said your dad was dead."

"He is." She squinted and let the smoke fall out of her mouth slowly, lips rounded into a little pink *O*. Her face seemed hazy through the blur of her own breath, and she reminded us of someone then, someone beautiful and baffling and gone—our mothers, our sisters, ourselves as we wished we could be.

"It gets a little old," she said.

IN THE WOODS at the edge of campus, when she felt the most alone? Or in her room, brushing her hair, the gauzy white-blond flurry smoothing out to something calm, his voice telling her how beautiful she looks? Or in the dark, beneath the covers, in that hard nighttime solitude that seems like it will never quit, until a whisper unravels from somewhere she can't place—inside herself, outside, all of it blending into this feeling of togetherness—is that what it was like? We couldn't stop imagining Lilith speaking to her dead father, this fact that trumped even the death of Mr. Arcilla. We were crazy with it, hopelessly jealous in ways we tried to hide but couldn't.

It never occurred to us not to believe her, and it doesn't seem right even now. We believed that she believed it, and that was enough to make it true.

"Like a voice, then?" Evie asked. "Like you can actually hear him talking to you?"

"No, not like a voice." Lilith was sprawled across her bed on top of Claire's thigh, feet dangling against Grace's shoulder, all her long hair spilled over the edge where Evie was braiding it slowly into her own. Middle of the night, and we were packed tight into her single as we often were after dorm lights-out, the empty quiet of our rooms driving us there just to feel the warmth of someone else breathing. Brains fuzzy with interrupted sleep. The dim light of street lamps outside and in the distance, barely, the glow of Boston like a mythic god we weren't allowed to touch. These were the times we felt most alive—pressed together in the dark, that vulnerable closeness we wouldn't allow ourselves during the day—yet every morning it would seem as if we had dreamt them, our nestled, blurry nights.

"But if it's not a voice," pushed Evie, "what exactly do you hear? And how can you be sure it's your dad?" Evie had no dad at all (or so she said), and we watched her expression for any sign of jealous fissure. But she kept her face carefully bored. Her raw, pink fingertips stitched delicately, plaiting her red ponytail into Lilith's white, the braided rope between them thickening, lengthening.

"I shouldn't have told you." Lilith's hands were stretched above her, working out the snags, and we could see the scars she never wanted to talk about—pale, parallel hatch marks in a row along the inner arm, ghosty lines tallying up so many things we didn't know about her. Sometimes she ran her fingers slowly up and down the row, and you could almost hear the sensation of skin against skin, like the high thrum of a delicate xylophone. "I don't know why you all keep asking. It's not like I can teach you how to do it." Her voice was tired, a little impatient, but even then we didn't believe she disliked the attention. We were old enough to know how good it felt, and to see it in another.

"Try," we said.

Her hands stopped in her hair, eyes closed. She pulled her arms down and folded them across her chest—tanned skin, thin wrists, tawny knot. "It's more like hearing the *sense* of something," she said. "Not the literal words, just the idea of them. Like an unwritten letter. Like that feeling when something's right on the tip of your tongue. I'll be holding a rock, about to skip it over the pond, and I'll sense his voice in my hand—like, *This is it, I know it*. And there it goes, twenty skips in a row. Or maybe the rock feels more like, *Not this time, babe*. And it sinks before I even try. Sometimes when we're sitting in chapel, I stick my gum under the pew and all of a sudden I know he saw me. He makes me *feel* it somehow, even if I don't hear the words exactly." She hesitated, eyes still closed and brow furrowed up. "Other times too. Like when I kissed Greg at the dance at Middlebrook. And I knew he was watching."

"You kissed Greg?"

"For real?"

"Greg who?"

"You never said you kissed Greg."

Our voices went buzzy with questions until Claire shushed us, nodding anxiously at the hallway. (Claire was the poorest of the Seven Sisters, with a full ride and the most to lose, which sometimes made her a good barometer of risk and other times a pain in the ass.) By the time we quieted, Lilith almost looked asleep, and we waited there, vigilant, for her to come back to life. "Every once in a while, it's more of a vision," she said finally. "Like of how he died. That's why I know he's dead, even though they keep telling me he's just gone—I keep seeing it happen, over and over, like he's showing me. He's in his car, and there's a bridge, and a river, and then a guardrail, and then everything goes black. I figure he must have skidded into the water somewhere. It would explain why his car disappeared at the same time." She opened her eyes and stared up at the ceiling. "See, it's not always a good thing."

But we thought it sounded pretty good. To have someone watching over you, to close your eyes and feel him there. To know what that was like.

"Is it just your dad?" Nellie asked from the end of the bed, her voice startling the rest of us—Nellie, who still had baby fat and braces and round cheeks of unpowderable shine, her body so frank and present we often forgot she was there. "Or do you think you could hear Mr. Arcilla too?"

Lilith didn't say anything. She just tilted her head at the ceiling, as if considering something, or deciding. Then she sat straight up. Her braid yanked Evie forward with her. But we all felt the pull.

"What if I *could* hear him?" she said. "What if he could tell us what really happened the night he died? And whoever was with him . . ." The orange lamplight outside the window splayed its corona around her head. We couldn't see her face anymore, just an eclipse of shadow, but we could hear it in her voice: the strange, bright promise of it, the gravity.

"If we do it right," she said, "maybe he could tell us who she really was."

THAT'S WHEN WE ALL STARTED LISTENING. In Mr. Arcilla's old classroom after dinner, slipping through the window during study hours to stand at his desk and touch the places he touched, our fingertips tented where he used to tent his own—waiting. Or reading aloud from our Spanish books, moving our tongues around the words he once pronounced for us, our eyes lingering on the photograph of a naked statue in Madrid: *Galatea y Su Escultor*. Holding the syllables against our lips and waiting for a feeling, a response, not sure what it was we wanted—a mouth against ours? Or someone to take the book from us, snap it closed?

In this way, through those middle weeks of fall, Mr. Arcilla was everywhere and nowhere all at once. In biology we drew the life cycle of butterflies, winged bodies arrowing through labeled loops: NYMPH. MOLT. RETURN. In algebra we changed the numbers we had known our whole lives into furtive letters and poked at their ghosts. Green trees began to tip with red, flushed themselves top to bottom. The sky unzipped the last of its summer lightning.

And always the pond. Edge of campus, beyond the bird sanctuary and the final row of faculty houses, in the shadows of a long line of willow trees that grazed their fingers across the surface. Off-limits to students, especially since that ill-fated dive, but we found ways to get there. All of us gathering after classes at the edge of the water in hopes of witnessing what we knew was bound to happen eventually: Mr. Arcilla reaching out to us, telling us the truth about what happened that night, and Lilith there to translate. We tried to hear him ourselves, of course, but in the end, we knew it would be her story to tell.

PROBLEM WAS, Mr. Arcilla was pretty quiet after his death. We tried not to lose faith in Lilith. But it was hard sometimes.

"Do you think it was a teacher who was with him?" she asked as we went through his desk drawers. Paper clips, Rolaids, an unsharpened pencil. Anonymous and bare, but we held them like talismans, charms of the dead.

"Why?" we asked her. "Are you getting a teacher vibe?"

"Maybe." She sounded doubtful. "But who would it have been?"

"Miss Ryan," offered Grace. "She's pretty."

Romy rolled her eyes. "Some things are more important than *pretty*, Grace." Though perhaps this wasn't true: our secret fear, and the reason we remember Romy's voice sounding angry. In a world where pretty mattered, Grace would be the likeliest survivor—Grace, who had fine black hair and doe eyes, who was a ballerina and moved like one, whose very name paved a life of elegant, effortless love. Grace was as beautiful as Lilith but didn't know it, which was the difference that made us all hate her a little—but especially Romy, who wanted more than anyone to be seen. "I never took Mr. Arcilla for shallow," she added, and her silver nose stud flashed indignantly.

"Well, it's not *just* that she's pretty," mumbled Grace. "I saw her crying the day we found out."

"We were all crying."

"Yes, but really crying, not group crying."

"I was thinking," Claire said quickly, ever the peace-keeper. "What if it was, like, someone's mom?" Which made Romy snort, which sparked Grace's giggles (we saw her doe eyes dart to Romy for approval), which set off Evie and even Nellie—the kind of laugh that kindles another one, which heightens the first, a laugh that isn't even about the joke but about the way it draws two laughs together. Claire shushed us ineffectually until Lilith held up her hand, nodding sternly at the closed door, and we stopped. She turned her back and ran her fingers through the chalkboard's ashy basin.

"Mr. Arcilla?" she said quietly. "It's Lilith and Romy and Evie. It's Claire and Nellie and Grace. Are you there?"

Our names, when Lilith said them, sounded slow and important as a magic spell. In her mouth we were an incantation.

"Can you hear us?"

But nothing turned into anything—no sound, no answer. Just Lilith's nails ghosting tracks in the bone-white chalk dust. Just the echo of our names, the Seven Sisters, the one missing.

LATER, AT THE POND, a new possibility: "Could it have been a student?"

It was hot that day, the kind of hot that has no place in crispy autumn, swimming-hole hot. We wanted more than anything to jump into the water. But Lilith said that was a desecration of a sacred space, so we sat along the bank and put our toes at the edge. Little lapping waves coming close, over and over, then moving away. Little tastes of what we really wanted.

"That's an interesting possibility," said Lilith, wrapping her arms around her knees. "An upper-school girl, you think? Couldn't have been much younger. And it wasn't any of us."

We nodded vigorously—*not us, not us*—as if defending ourselves. We didn't need to; we had all been in Lilith's bedroom the night Mr. Arcilla died, Lilith reading us the dirty parts from an Ovid text she'd stolen from a prefect. But a defense felt necessary all the same. Maybe because of the way that night was tinged with shame when we thought back to it—the warm lamplight of her room and the sound of her voice, the sound of the poetry like a hand in the dark, and somewhere at the same time, Mr. Arcilla sinking under the weight of so much water.

("The nymph was spellbound," she had read aloud, "burning with passion." The way she'd looked at us then, unblinking: how we couldn't look back for too long. "And her eyes now were as bright as sunlight, reflected in a mirror.")

Here at the pond, we still couldn't look at her. We watched the unsettled flicker of the water, but from the edge of the shine we could see Lilith smiling a weird smile. "You want it to be you, is that it?" she said finally, and she could have been speaking to any of us, could have been speaking to all of us. "The one we're all looking for. The last person who saw him before he died, the last person he kissed. The person of interest."

Claire flushed and shook her head: *No. No.* Evie picked at her nonexistent nails, Romy scowled at the pond, Grace stared prettily at the passing clouds with false attention. Only Nellie looked back at Lilith, looked right into her eyes with a watery gaze and illegible expression, her arms folded tight across the waistband of the unflattering uniform we all wore, and which we were grateful Nellie wore worst. But even Nellie, eventually, looked away.

Lilith shook her head, hugged her knees tighter. "A girl—a *student.*" All her pale hair fell forward, hiding her face. "Could he have been that kind of man? Did we really not know him at all?"

IN HER BEDROOM, days later, we found the last chapter he had tried to teach us: *ser* versus *estar,* two separate ways of being. We'd had trouble with that one from the start. But as Lilith read aloud to us, as we tried to hear his voice in hers, it suddenly made as much sense as anything.

How does she feel?

She is calm.

Ella está tranquila.

What is she like?

She is secretive.

Ella es reservada.

The condition of the thing, or the essence of the thing. The layer on top, or the truth underneath. She held the book lightly in her hands and stopped after a while, and we all sat there in a silence that felt beautiful—tranquil and reserved—understanding for the first time two different ways of being. We leaned against each other, watched the clouds slide by the open window, our bare feet touching on the bed. The pages fluttering between Lilith's long, still fingers: a stirring.

"What if it was a man?" Lilith asked.

We hadn't said this out loud before. It was not what we had agreed upon, this version of the story that left no space for us, that made an older version of ourselves anything but the right answer. We didn't speak, and the silence was no longer tranquil, but what it was, we couldn't name.

Lilith looked at us and frowned. "Well, it's just as possible, isn't it?"

Yes, we said, looking away. It was a possibility.

"And we don't have any other leads, do we?"

No, we admitted, we don't.

A long pause clenched the room. Then she flopped facedown on her pillow and sighed into it. "Well, I don't know what to do anymore," she said, voice muffled. "We're not getting anywhere with this. You aren't any help at all. And trying is just making everything worse." She was suddenly fighting back tears, we could hear the chokes, and our hands were quick on her hair, her arms—this was something we did well, this collective comforting—until Romy took over and rubbed her back in slow circles. That first year, when a wall broke down, we were good at building it back up for each other. We all wanted to be next in line. This was not about succession, though perhaps it seems that way now, when we close our eyes and watch the memory of Romy smoothing slow, invisible circles into Lilith's white shirt, like a gently erased page of paper.

"What's wrong, Lilith? What's wrong?"

Lilith sniffled into the pillow, an ugly sound, guttural and wet. Then she slapped Romy's hand away and rolled onto her side. "Don't you get how hard this is? I can't hear Mr. Arcilla. He isn't *there*. I'm trying, I really am, I promise. But I don't think it works for just anyone." Her knees were curling up to her chest, her fingers covering up her face. Her whole body folded into itself like a letter. "I'm telling you, the more I try to hear him, the more I just hear my dad. And he won't fucking leave me *alone*."

We still flinched a little at curse words, but Lilith could wield them like knives.

"It's like he's everywhere," she said, "all the time. Reminding me how he's not here. Reminding me how I don't know what happened to him, not really. Like the bridge—that's still there, and the water, and the guardrail, and it starts out the same as it's always been. But half the time he doesn't die at all. He just keeps driving. And I'll be looking for Mr. Arcilla, I'll be trying so hard to hear him, but all I can see is this big winding road, and I don't know where it goes, and it's driving me *crazy*."

She was crying harder, breath coming in loud, wet hitches, hands pressed against her ears. We were used to this, but from each other. Not from Lilith. We met each other's eyes and read them wordlessly. We moved closer on the bed, circling her.

It's only now that we can ask: Was there something thrilling about seeing her cry? Something good—we would never have admitted it, never have said it out loud—in seeing her not so different from our secret, late-night selves?

"The scariest thing," she said, and her voice was so quiet, "is what if I'm making the whole thing up? What if all he did was leave?" And we felt the tears pricking hot in our eyes, and we squeezed them back. "If he isn't dead at all, then what does that make *me*?"

The tight little tangle of her. The knotted arms, the mussed hair, the jumble of hands and legs in the dark, aching to be undone—maybe that's why we needed her so much. Maybe we believed that figuring out Mr. Arcilla meant figuring out Lilith, and figuring out Lilith meant figuring out ourselves.

AND MAYBE, IN THE END, that's why we took her to the pond. One of those dreamy, street-lamped nights in her room, and we asked her, Why not? The water is the closest you can get to him, right? And she said, No, it's finished, I want to stop. And we said, Don't you want to try? No. Just to see what it's like? No. Just once? And she started to cry. Just to find out, we said, rubbing her back, and then we can be done. And she looked away from us, out the window, for a very long time. Then she said yes.

Down the fire escape and into the shivering night. Across the hillside and into the woods. We walked along the bank single file, everywhere around us the crunching sounds of fall and that first silvery sharpness in the air, that hint of the winter to come. But it was easy to ignore it, to feel instead the warm bloom of walking in that group toward some kind of revelation, everyone hoping the same things together. Stepping in each other's footprints, reaching out to balance ourselves against another girl. A small, wordless laugh in the darkness. "The Seven Sisters," said Romy, pointing up at the stars, the Pleiades linked in their steadfast alliance. "Most of the time you can only see six. But in the fall, on the clearest nights, the seventh star comes out." And we searched the sky for her, that lost sister in her holding pattern, circling. We followed Lilith to what we thought was the right place, and it felt the whole way like we had been here before.

It must have been midnight by the time we reached the long wooden dock. Reedy and grassy on both sides, the pond black beyond it, one cool slice of moon floating in the water. Lilith walked ahead of us, silhouetted against the surface, and stopped at the end of the dock, looking out. "Is this it?" she asked.

We stayed behind, watching her. We reached for each other's hands. "You tell us," we said.

The silence of that moment. Only the lapping of the surface, the secrets underneath. Lilith took a deep breath and didn't let go, just held it inside and looked across the water at something we couldn't see. Tilting her head like she always did (even now it's how we picture her), listening to something we couldn't hear. Her nightgown billowed, bright in the dim light, and lacy—the old-fashioned kind, with a little silk rosette in the middle of the breastbone—and the loose, fluttering breeze of her blond hair curled at the edges. She couldn't have looked any more like a little girl, lost. Waiting for someone to remember her.

And the rest of us? What did we want right then, what was it *we* were waiting for? If we close our eyes now, what haunts us is the mirror of that moonlit pond. How leaning over and looking in could turn you briefly into someone you were not—the ripples, the starlight gleam, a body warped and beautiful and older and other, as mysterious and almost there as the lover we were looking for. Something that felt like an answer to the question we've never stopped asking. *Who was she? Who was she?* We can tell you this: what we wanted back then was a name. So why is it that standing there, our hands laced together, our eyes catching on the slope of Lilith's cheek as it turned away from us, our mouths still heavy with Mr. Arcilla's Spanish words—*deseo, pérdida, muerte*—still, despite everything, all we could think of was the faraway feeling of home?

Lilith slipped one strap down over her shoulder, quickly, thoughtlessly, and it was our mother brushing a strand of hair off her neck.

She let the nightgown fall to her ankles, and it was our father dropping his jacket to the floor, then stepping away.

The skinny little slip of her. The birdlike bones, the tender and breakable fact of her body, and suddenly there we were, each one of us, at the end of the dock—fragile and alone, just as we had known ourselves to be all along.

She looked back at us once and smiled, as if to say: *This is it, I know it.*

Or as if to say: *Not this time, babe.*

It's a tricky thing, translation. We never had an ear for it.

Then she fell into the water, quick and deep to a place we couldn't see. And didn't come up for a long time.

THERE ARE CERTAIN THINGS we don't let ourselves remember.

We don't remember how long we waited there, the seconds seeming endless, the ripples smoothing out to stillness. The unspoken, unbroken blank of the water, like an empty page of paper. And how Lilith never came up to mark it.

We don't remember how long it was until someone screamed, and how suddenly all of us were screaming. How unbroken that was too, at least for a while—all the screams weaving into each other, all the separate voices becoming one before they scattered in the night. We don't remember who jumped in and dragged her from the bottom, although we know it was one of us, or maybe all of us. And we don't remember the color of her face—the stony white of it, impossible white, like marble or undone magic, a Spanish statue frozen in a text-book photograph—before we pressed the water out of her and kissed her breathing back to life.

We don't remember how long it took for campus security to come, though we do remember that it was long enough to help her back into her nightgown. Long enough to crowd close and hold her, fold our arms into a single human blanket while she shivered at the center. How we tried to re-create those nestled dorm-room nights—the braiding, the lamplight, the Ovid we passed from hand to hand. But she wouldn't look at us. Her teeth chattered a little, but otherwise that marble stillness, that foreigner silence.

We don't remember, we don't let ourselves remember, the ride to Headmistress Salk's house, or the way she came rushing down the stairs breathlessly, a flowery red robe ballooning behind her, hair set in curlers, no makeup on—as mundane and unpolished and beautiful as we had ever seen her, sweeping Lilith up in her wide, warm arms. "You're okay," she said, "you're okay." And Lilith was crying then, and so was the headmistress, and after a while Mr. Salk came down the stairs and put his arms around both of them. They ran their hands over Lilith's hair, the clumpy mess of it, like cut ropes hanging down from her neck. "You're okay, sweet girl, you're okay."

And no, of course we don't remember what that felt like. To watch it from across the room. Our own hair damp and cold against our skin, and no one to untangle it.

We never did learn what happened to Mr. Arcilla. There were rumors, of course, and there still are occasionally—murmurs at alumni meetings of his secret alcoholism, of a drug deal gone wrong. Brief speculation about a tedious affair with the registrar's wife. Polished little pebbles of stories we've heard before, and we pass them along from girl to girl like we dutifully pass along news of marriages and children. After a while they jumble together in the same way we all have—a name, a blurred detail, a friendship we swore was unshakable plunking down, one by one, into that dark abyss of memory. Who's to say we'd recall the specifics of his death even if we knew them? You never know what's going to sink, what's going to stay. You never know what's going to keep returning all your life, lapped up on the shores of later selves.

It doesn't matter. What matters, what comes back to us, is the way Lilith looked up tearfully into the faces of the Salks. What we remember is her stone-cold lie, her hard and steady voice, a voice that didn't match her tears when she said to them: "It was me. I was there with Mr. Arcilla the night he died. He sent me a note, he asked me to meet him, and—" Her words cutting short, as if she couldn't tell them the rest. What we remember is the way they stared at each other, horrified, then tender, and how they swooped down again, holding her even more forcefully against them, shushing in her ear. "Quiet now, dear. Quiet. It's over. It's over." And what we can't forget: her dark eyes looking out from beneath their embrace, across the room at the rest of us, the sweet and bitter taste of that look before she turned away and left for home and we never saw her again.

A Myth of Satellites

———— ❧ ————

ROLL BACK TIME like the blanket it is and you can still see them, those summer nights of fourteen years old. The way the sky was a body freckled with stars, beautiful in a way that felt cruel. Impossibly human and impossibly far.

That summer was the summer of Romy. New girl in Coralville, town that never moved forward, had always been moving in the same unchecked orbit: town of ice cream with dusty friends after baseball games. Town of beer games with hopeless friends after ice cream. Town of icy beer on baseball fields gone hopeless with dust. Town of circling and circling the bases, of one-two-three-out, town you would never send sailing, never hero your way out of.

Impossible, then, that she chose you, this girl with the dark magic eyes and the pixie cut, the dimples that emptied your gut of breath. Yet there she was at your kitchen door, telescope in hand, mosquitoes swirling porch-light orange around her head. The first night she appeared, your mother dropped a whole pot of soup at your father's feet, scalding him. You heard the gasp. You looked up from the table and saw your mother first (her sway, the sucked breath, pot loosening in her grip) and then your father's face fisting in rage at the burn, a scowl that would have made you look down if not for the fact that your mother didn't. She just kept staring at the door, and only then did you notice the girl's silhouette behind it, one hand pressed against the screen.

"Anne," your mother said. Calmly, in a regular voice, as if calling her in for dinner.

Of course it wasn't Anne. But for a moment time funneled, zoomed in like a spun lens, and you thought so too. The hiss of her nails on the knitted metal. Bleached-blond haircut haloing gold, and the combat boots, the glinty insolence of a silver nose ring. How the soup splayed in the air as it fell, a hot constellation: the awareness of something about to burn you before it lands.

She pressed her hand harder—Romy, not Anne—and the screen flexed inward and your father left the room. "Elijah," she said, looking past your mother. Looking straight, impossibly, at you. "It's been a long time."

The night sky behind her sitting up and leaning in.

ROMY TAUGHT YOU STARS THAT SUMMER. *Celestial bodies,* she called them. You remember that phrase in her mouth, you're almost sure. Maybe it's the reason you still see the sky as freckled, fragile, a lover in the dark. A body always rolling away.

She brought her telescope to your deck that night, and every night after until school began. Never her house—you understood that early, a brittle look she gave you at the suggestion, and you didn't ask why. For a while just the trade of the telescope, skinny black barrel of it warming in your fingers, hands brushing if you weren't careful. Leaning, in a way that you hoped seemed offhand, against the dry-rot railing that was painted white once but had long ago faded. Long nights, few words. You paid for it. Punished each morning with the memory of mosquitoes, red thumbprints along your skin. Punished with imagined things you could have said to her—quips, charming and funny, always ideas that came too late. Punished with your father's pointed silence and the questioning looks your mother gave you at breakfast, wanting something—some report, some truth—that felt too insubstantial to hand over when you weren't even sure what it was.

She wasn't really pretty, for example. The flat chest and piercings, the deep-cut dimples, the dark freckles that mottled her face—you knew none of this matched what you understood *pretty* to mean. *Pretty* was curvy. *Pretty* was long, soft hair and pink lips and doll-bright eyes and doll-pale skin. Romy was none of these things. And yet *pretty* is what came into focus, adjusting its contours.

She wasn't really new, either, because nothing in Coralville is ever really new. Turns out she'd grown up on the other side of town. Same year as you, but she'd gone to a different elementary. Then boarding school in Boston, which hadn't worked out (she slid her eyes away, left it at that), and now a move across town, a new house, new district. "My dad calls it a fresh start," she said. "But it's not really, because I remember you. We used to play at the park when we were, like, five. You built forts with me, remember? Once, you reached over and pulled a scab off my knee. That's why I knew to come here."

You were mortified at that, so heart-thumping dumb you couldn't even ask her to explain what she meant. (And yet beneath it, even still, wasn't there something delicious in a memory you weren't sure you had? That you were making right then? The deep, inexplicable satisfaction of the scab lifting. The new blood underneath—slow to come into color, then surging to Polaroid brightness as you watched.)

In the meantime, stars. Her dad taught cosmology at the observatory, she said. The big one in Iowa City. That's how she knew so much about space, about celestial bodies. "The constellations too," she added, adjusting the telescope. "Unscientific as they are. Although when you think about it, astronomy is just as mythic as astrology."

She didn't speak like other girls you knew. Other girls spoke in questions: high, fluttery loops of uncertainty. Romy spoke in answers, even if you hadn't asked the questions.

"For instance"—she squinted into the eyepiece—"all the light that comes from stars is already dead, billions of years old. What we're looking at is history. It doesn't even exist anymore."

"I know that already," you said. "That's, like, the biggest cliché about stars."

Why did you sound so angry? It wasn't how you felt. You could see your mother watching from behind the curtain, letting it fall closed when you shot her a glare. But even then the gray outline of her body behind it, waiting.

"All the time, people think they see something actually happening," Romy said. "Supernovas, shooting stars—we think they mean something. We wish on them. But it's never real. It's never *now*."

"Yeah, I get it."

She glanced up from the telescope. In the dark, her eyes were black holes. One side of her face was a white crescent arc, the other side inscrutable. "You think you get it," she said. "But you haven't looked, have you?"

A DREAM, THAT FIRST NIGHT, OF ANNE. Not how she was in real life, but how she was in the posters—prim blouse buttoned high, smile shiny with braces. Her face hadn't Xeroxed well, half-blacked by shadow. But you papered the neighborhood with her anyway, stapled your grayscale sister to hundreds of phone poles: *Missing. Missing. Missing.* Once, you'd used these same poles as stickball bases. Once, they'd meant nothing other than *Safe!* In your dream your mother stopped and stared at the poster, the photograph she herself had chosen, and said, *It doesn't even look like her now.* (This was true, of course. Because where was the chin jutting in defiance, the ear cuffs and belly ring always on display, the boys' arms looped like necklaces around her throat? The truth was, they wanted the other Anne back, the one with braces and blouses.) And your father said, *What does it matter? Everyone knows what she looks like. Every goddamn square inch of her.* And your mother slapped him, and your father cried, and then they held each other for so long, you had to look away, up at the pole where the stapled posters rustled and flapped like lifted skirts. You pressed yourself against home base, told yourself you'd pin her down if you could only reach.

You haven't looked, Romy said, *have you?* But that was the thing about her. Every memory of that summer, every memory of Romy, is a memory of touch, taste, smell—so rarely a memory of seeing. You barely remember what she looked like, or if you do, it's a hazy memory sharpened only by her yearbook photograph, a black-and-white half smile smudged by decades of opening and closing. What you remember is tactile. You remember how all the pieces of the telescope stacked smoothly into themselves like nesting dolls. You remember dusk dissolving gauzily to dark, quick as sugar on the tongue. Sometimes Romy would step back and sigh, jutting her chin skyward in search of a constellation that wasn't where it was supposed to be, her body rigid with frustration—then a sudden, fluid loosening when she found what she was looking for and whirled the telescope in that direction. And what you remember of all this is not how she looked but how that loosening felt in your own bones. Dark boom of the telescope swinging through the night, the sensation of moving forward.

Once, you reached out to touch her cropped hair as she leaned over the eyepiece, stopped yourself before your fingers met the surface. And yet even after you pulled back your hand, you had the memory in your skin of what it felt like, that frayed corn silk. You knew it would smell musky like bedsheets, that it would tickle your neck in a way you would love and hate, although you had never touched it before and never would.

When she glanced up, her eyes lingered on your hand, and you wondered if she'd felt you pull away. You felt a flush burning just beneath the skin of your neck, meaty and hot: shame, desire, indistinguishable. You waited for her to call you out. But she just smiled. "I bet you were always the good kid," she said. "Weren't you?" The look she gave you then: crystalline-bright taste of lemons, though you couldn't say why.

THAT SUMMER WAS the last summer of your old life, the life in which you were Elijah. Elijah was the gawky, awkward boy still oh-for-twenty on the season, too tall and trippy for soccer tryouts. Body like a bottle rocket gone suddenly screwy. Elijah was the boy no one would snowball with at the last middle school dance, not even shiny-faced Trista with chub rub and psoriasis. The kid mothers shook their heads about with sympathy over casseroles in other houses, houses with homemade noodles and pot roast and two parents who talked, houses without canned soup and Hungry-Man stacked in the freezer like corpses. Elijah was the boy whose sister ran away from home two years ago. Whose last name, no matter what he did, would make the high school teachers look up, pause, and look away.

The last name—you could do nothing about that.

But Elijah you could tamp down. You could rise above him. High school the last blank space in front of you, and when the bell rang on the first day of the ninth grade, when the class settled down and the teacher called your name and paused, you would have a way to fill the awful silence. *It's Jay,* you would tell them. *I go by Jay.*

So that's who you would be. Jay. The flight of the word from behind your teeth, cool and quick as a hollow-boned bird. You tried to hold that feeling in your mind during those long summer afternoons, photographing things that didn't move, waiting for night to come, waiting for Romy and stars, and already you could feel your life loosening, snapping the ropes of some earthbound tether. The airy blue float of a new name: the sort of boy who would circle above it all.

THIS UNLEASHING WAS easier in your mind. In the real world, the sticky press of reality held you down—that endless hangover of summer days, blank and unchanging, always squeezing inward at the edges.

Afternoons at Luke's house by the falling-down playground you'd conquered as children. Drinking Milwaukee's Best with Luke's older brother, Brent, like you had all summer, like it felt you would (you couldn't tell if you hoped this or feared it) until the end of time. You took turns with the empty beer cans, pinging them with the BB gun Luke's mom hated—*Just you watch,* she liked to say, *you'll put out an eye*—the sun smudging heat up the wavering blacktop, the park going ghosty. Like your stories about Romy. How they swelled up a little in the daylight, wobbled, only half-recognizable. Like Brent's wet voice, over and over, a woozy slur: "When in Rome, man, when in Rome, when in Rome."

"What does that even mean?" you said.

"Watch this," Luke said, took aim, and missed again.

"It means do as the Romys do." Brent nodded, his acne burns

seething and sweaty. "I heard she fucked a teacher at her boarding school. They kicked her out."

"No," said Luke. "I heard it was the hockey team."

Brent sighed and leaned back in his lawn chair, the frayed yellow nylon straining. "Eli, man, she's *asking* for it. You should *tap* that." As if she were a source to be harnessed, a magical potion to drink from. And maybe it did feel that way. That summer was like one endless, imminent arrival, the man you would become just over the noon-bleached horizon, though you tried to conjure him faster with Brent and beer and the gun's tunnel vision. Hanging with Brent—his thick, ropy biceps, his goatee the color of drought grass—felt like hanging with an adult, though he'd graduated from high school only a year ago. Anne's year. He'd dated Anne in middle school; you remembered him coming to wait for her at the end of your driveway, and in your memory he was an adult even then, same heavy-lidded gaze, eyes silver-blue as BBs. And yet you understood that this middle school version of Brent in your memory was younger than you were right now, about to start at Coralville High.

Something about this tangle of time—memory interlacing with things that hadn't happened yet, old you and future you in the same place—was why you couldn't stop making up stories that summer. Some of them stayed in your head, like what if Anne had never dumped Brent, which would mean she'd still be here, and he wasn't so bad, was he? Some of them winged free, loosed themselves in front of Brent and Luke, who ogled as you conjured the specter of Romy before them. Exaggerating, maybe, the way she looked at you, the way she leaned in close. What she suggested you do in the dark. But only a little.

"Sweet girl," said Brent, toasting you with a beer. "Maple sugar ass. And knows, apparently, how to share. Tap, tap, tap, my friend."

"Here's one," Luke said, bringing you a bullet-ridden can, middle flayed open. "Good and gutted."

You told him thanks. Positioned it on the edge of the picnic table, right on the border of sunlight and shade, and pulled out your camera.

"Why do you do that anyway, taking all those pictures?" said Brent. Even his voice was thick; he belched through the phlegm. "Just empty cans."

You shrugged and tilted closer, searching out the right angle. Brain slack now with beer and the cool drift of a night you had to look forward to that they did not. "Something to do," you said. The jagged edges made interesting shadows on the table—you zoomed in and the shadows gnashed their teeth, stretched like claws. A turn of the lens and the world dilated to meaninglessness, then back again to meaning, a monster made and unmade at your will.

"When in Romy, when in Romy, when in Romy," Brent said.

AT SOME POINT, a scratching sound in your dream: Was it then, or is it now? You are eleven years old, in bed, and your mother has locked the screen door again as a lesson. The scratching on the metal is a signal to you, a cry in the night across a darkened bedroom. Comforting somehow—because you know what to do, you are useful and needed and Anne calls and you go to her. Unlock the door and let her in. Sometimes she is giggling. Sometimes she is crying. Either way, her nighttime voice is swirly and grateful, her sudden hug a crushing warmth. *EJ, my buddy, my buddy. You are the best.* She stumbles, smells of earth and sweat and bodies and beer, a blurry silhouette as she moves to her room, and in this dream she hasn't yet left home forever. She hasn't packed her one suitcase with every last scrap of clothing, hasn't written on her mirror in lipstick, *Don't come looking.* In this dream, none of it has happened, all the things that will happen in the morning, every morning: your father's shouts at breakfast. Your mother burning oatmeal. Your sister's eyes still gritty with makeup, sleep-smudged but sparkly, like half-tromped snow. Her gaze that cold. You eat your cornflakes, and the crunch drowns out the yelling. You wash the bowl, scrape the oatmeal crud from the pan, swirl the dish soap around and around and around until it's clean, the kitchen empty, the morning purged and silent and spinning down the drain.

Predictable, this dream, as it was predictable then. Each scene like a point on a graph chart in math class, or a constellation adding up to some ancient and decipherable meaning. A pattern was there once, whether you recognized it or not, and in the dreams you can squint your eyes, watch for a clue you missed until it all falls into order. You peer deep into the black space of it every night.

ROMY WAS THE FIRST PERSON you showed the photographs to, or at least the first person who really *saw* them. The magnified, shot-up beer cans. The knife cuts on trees. A dead bird so enlarged that it lost the sense of itself, just an abstract pattern of shapes and downy shadows. The pictures were secret because the pictures didn't match who you were: the boy next door who played JV baseball, who got good grades in algebra, who never made his parents worry. You handed her the stack with shaking hands, light on the deck going faded and dusky, and she looked at them for a long time, her blond head dipped low and still, so long your racing heart had time to slow down. So long that you were sure, suddenly, she was faking her attention, couldn't possibly still be interested. She was making fun of you. A flash of anger: a need to hold something, hit it hard against something else. But then she looked up.

"They're incredible," she said. "Beautiful, but violent. Like you're pushing my face into the world and making me see things I wouldn't look at otherwise."

The clench of your stomach letting go. Insides loopy and wild as moths flinging themselves against the deck light. You were already in love with her, of course. But that was the moment you recognized the feeling, and you would have given her anything then, any closely held truth, precious and shiny, any answer to a question she could ask. *Why do you do that anyway, taking all those pictures?* You wanted her to ask it, and you would have offered her a thousand answers: Because there is something real about the can's emptiness, the way it becomes even more real in the photograph. Because evidence. Because cause and effect. Because your mother's shredded cuticles and your father still staring at the phone, even now, even decades later, when he pretends to watch TV. Because when you found this camera left behind in Anne's closet, you thought that it might be enough—to look through those zooming tunnels, to see what she must have seen.

Because Romy herself, her cool, distant light, impossible and possible all at once.

But she didn't say anything else. She just smiled at your dumb, missed-shot smile (this was the moment you could have asked *her* a question, not waited for one, you know that now, the moment you could have changed everything and didn't), and then she turned away. The telescope in her hands unspooled, tripod clawing open. You could sense her about to launch into space, into meaningless talk of dwarf planets and myths, and you felt a desperate urge to yank her back to earth and hold her down. "Could I photograph you sometime?" you asked. Heard it aloud even before you thought it.

Romy laughed. "Are you saying I'm beautiful and violent?" She didn't look at you, didn't answer your question. She just looked into the telescope, dusk going electric blue around her as she fiddled with the settings. After a long time she said, "Andromeda's out tonight. There's your photo. They said she was too pretty and chained her to a rock as punishment. For a sea monster to eat. Poseidon did that, I think, or maybe her father." She tilted her head, aimed the lens. "Look," she said.

That taste in your mouth: something gone stale. That beating of wings down deep in your chest that was only, always, stupidly, your heart. "The stars aren't even out yet."

"But I know it's coming."

Something in her voice then reminded you of Brent—the way he was still waiting for Anne at the end of your mind's driveway, both older and younger at the same time. Something that was over even as it was arriving: the darkening sky, the courage to kiss her, the rap on the window, your mother's signal for bed. How you watched her get smaller and smaller every night as she walked down the street-lamped road toward home. That time in your life, though you didn't know it yet, was everything about to happen and everything already over. High school a new inning, hopeful rumble in the stands, and summer nothing more than the same old strike right past you.

IF YOU WANTED TO, you could remember it this way: the night-time grass icy beneath your hot skin, your bodies so alive, lying side by side looking up at dead stars. Romy could have raised her hand and traced patterns into meaning: Cepheus, Perseus, dippers tipping back and forth into each other. She could have put her arm back down and it would have been next to yours, freckled skin glowing in the night, a flickering current beside you. She could have leaned in, leaned over you, all the wild static in your body finding, finally, the focal point of her mouth, the long, dark emptiness of her body flung ecstatic into bright light, blinding as a flash. Sometimes you let yourself remember it this way. The image curls at first like a bent photograph, and your mind smooths it down. The image sharpens. Don't tell me you see something different.

WHAT IS IT about adulthood that misses its own arrival? The headlights of that summer cut off quick as a car on a distant freeway and suddenly it's October, suddenly you're looking back and wondering what happened, how you got here, to this life you thought you wanted—Jay, this new sound that felt exactly the same.

Same loops of chatter in the cafeteria.

Same sock-smelling bus home.

That crunch on the dusty gravel of your life, those same tireless circles.

The lockers, at least, were different—longer and wider than the middle school's, as if there was some acknowledgment that high school meant more baggage. You liked to run your hands down the row of locks between classes, on a bathroom pass in the empty hallways, spin the dial you knew to be Romy's when no one was around. Sometimes anonymous lockers too, any one of them Anne's, any spin a combination that could have once belonged to her. That thought had been a comfort before you were actually here.

But now you could see these lockers weren't really that different. The same gunshot bangs, the same beige, blank, unyielding metal.

And Romy, slammed just as abruptly shut. Your nighttime deck filling slowly with leaves and the stars left unstoried; she was an unexplained absence one night at the screen door, and suddenly, she never came again. You still saw her in school, moon-bright and visible in any hallway—your eyes always seeking her out in a crowd—and sometimes she met your gaze at the end of a dark tunnel of faces, and sometimes she didn't. She spent most of her time in the red-carpet hall, a long line of senior lockers most underclassmen avoided but that you had to cross to walk to English. You'd steal glimpses of her then, some lanky senior arm coiled around her shoulders, tanned skin, sandy hair, same guy, different guy, didn't matter. They spun around her like satellites, always another one waiting at the edge, all tangled in orbit around this shiny new thing you'd been foolish enough to think you could keep.

A myth of satellites, she told you once, *is that they are circling in space. Really, they are endlessly falling.*

That's what it felt like. Endlessly falling. Your father's fungoes after practice, each one just beyond your glove's reach. Your mother's eyes cast lower at the dinner table: *And what happened to Romy, then? Haven't seen her in ages.* The tumble-dark laughter of seniors, jostling you over the threshold of a classroom: *Are you lost, Frosh?* Trip of your feet, tangle of your ankles, Brent handing you another beer and another, until even that wasn't enough, craving something stronger to make you forget the taste of summer—*Easy, man,* Brent said, *pace yourself. Gunning for fall-down drunk if you don't watch out.*

Even Romy herself—hadn't she merely fallen into something she would have laughed at weeks ago, the suck of high school hierarchy? You thought of helpless moons yanked into the tracks of planets, dust motes riding the easiest current. In your kinder moments, you gave her credit for mere powerlessness. A freshman girl suckered in by the fawning seniors. You could hardly blame her.

In less kind moments, an empty feeling, gutted as a can. She hadn't even said goodbye.

Eventually, snow. Early storm that fall and a cold snap that made it stay. The deck draped with a white sheet, and you looked over it late at night sometimes, icy with the Popov you asked Brent to buy with his fake ID. You liked the clear, cool escape of it, the name: *Popov.* A better name than blue, feathery Jay. Popov was Russian, brusque, sharper than the vague bubbliness of beer, a drink that now seemed girlish and weak. You liked your mind colder than that. Bright and dangerous, white with static like falling snow.

YOU COULD STOP THERE. You could let Romy float off into whiteness—this occurs to you now, decades later, watching the snow falling outside, the horizon plush and unnaturally soft in a way that is possible only at night, only with snow falling silently. A pinkish and fragile sky: life gathering sweetly these days when you least expect it. The way beauty can hold you hostage with fear. You feel like that when you look at your daughter, who is still pinkish and fragile herself, porcelain fine, and swaddled so tight in the next room that you think she can't possibly breathe. But your wife tells you no, babies like the feeling of constraint, faith that the world still wraps itself around them in a way that is safe and shielding and can't you let her believe that just a little while longer? Before time throws back the covers?

Even now, just weeks old, and already they're slapping your back at work saying, *Beautiful.* Saying, *Aren't you in trouble, Jay.* Saying, *Lock her up quick, lock her up!*

Saying, *Aw. Look at her.*

Remembering suddenly, in that pink snowy night at the end of the line called now, a photograph of a stripped bed. Luke passing it to you, or maybe Brent, faces flickering, another party, another Saturday night made electric at the edges, and laughter too, flailing out of someone's throat like a shot bird—yours? Hard to tell, just the grate of it like a shiver, joyous and shocking at once: nails dragged on a screen. *Check it out,* someone is saying. *Jay, you gotta check it out, will you look at this shit,* and you feel your vision zoom, have to concentrate to do this, slow-spin the drunken aperture of your eyes down to the photograph in your hands. A bed, a body. Two bodies. Three bodies—are your eyes blurring yet? So hard to focus because it's all layering together in the picture: the long white current of her body, naked on a bare mattress. That blue silky fabric that mattresses are made of, electric blue like the sky just after dusk, shiny in a way you can feel in your fingertips. The dark point of her tit—*areola,* you

know now, you have that word now, but then you had only *tit*—dark
and red like a bullet hole shot into the white. *When in Romy, man,
when in Romy!* someone is saying, again and again until it has no
meaning. *Dude, she's so tanked. Look at her, she's tapped.* Other bodies
at the edges of the frame, monstrous: darker slice of someone between
her legs, someone who was never you. And someone else is grabbing
it away even now, before you can see the rest, a hairy hand crumpling
the picture, or maybe that's another hand inside the picture—hard
to tell what's inside and what's outside—and there's a feeling in your
gut like a screen door swinging, moths against a light, the need to
throw something against something else, there's a voice coming out
of you—*Full throttle,* your dad used to say about Anne, and what's
that memory doing here?—and you can hear other voices now saying
Chill, Jay, saying *Fuck, man,* and you're laughing and crumpling and
throttling and chilling, the whole hot mess of it fading out, if you let
it, if you'll just fucking let it happen, man, back to white.

THERE WERE TIMES THEN, as there are times now, when you
tried to shove your mind onto the blank white page of the day before
Anne left home. Tried to make an imprint, a mark, a wet, dark
smudge—anything as long as it was *something.* A cruel word you said
to her the day before. A way you met her eyes, pitying, that made her
pause, hair brushed half out of her face, and consider what you saw
when you looked at her. An invitation she floated to you, hopeful—
Want to watch a movie, EJ? Want to play checkers?—that you denied,
turning away, tired of being on guard against the flare of her temper,
tired of being the good kid. Or a scratching at the door you heard and
didn't answer, pressed down with the stifle of a white pillow. What
you wanted was a path from A to B, a pattern of dots taking shape—
something to interpret. What you wanted more than anything (and

this is a horrible want, the kind of hunger that becomes its own black hole, that eats even its own emptiness) was to be the cause of something. The last out of the game, the apology. Because then you would, at least, be in charge of the story. You would pack it into itself like a nesting-doll monster, the worst story you could tell, the worst thing you could have said to her, and the whole thing would be neat and contained and horrible and tellable and there you would be, no longer on the sidelines, holding the ending in your own hands.

But what it won't stop becoming is the truth: you have no idea what you said to Anne the day before she ran away. You have no memory of it because the day she left, you didn't think to think of it. The day she left was only the vivid, face-grabbing insistence of *today*—Anne missing after school, through dinner, late into the night without a call, the police finally arriving, the short-lived belief that perhaps she had been taken. *Kidnapped:* a familiar story, a narrative you all understood. (Only later would you recognize how sweet and easy this time was, the brief period in which you all thought she was a victim. That she would want to be found.) The police asked you questions, but the questions were all about today, only today, and your mother served oozy lemon bars as if it were a very sad dinner party, and though you didn't want one, you ate the whole thing like you knew you should.

It wasn't until the next morning that someone thought to look in her dresser, which was empty; that someone else noticed the missing suitcase, the lipstick scrawl on the makeup mirror; that her role changed. And by then it was too late. You didn't remember to think of *yesterday* until yesterday's details had sunk too far beneath the surface to retrieve them.

You know they're still there. They drift sometimes through the black of dreams, that nighttime abyss, brush your skin like monstrous tentacles that could grab you (aren't you always waiting for them to grab you?) yet never do. They leave you only to imagine the dark possibilities. For instance: that whatever unknown thing you said was the nudge that sent her out the door. Or somehow worse: that whatever you said didn't matter at all. That it's not something you would change if you could, that it's exactly what you would say now if you had the chance to do it over, and still it wasn't enough to make her stay, and still everything that has already happened will happen again and again.

NIGHT BEFORE ROMY LEFT TOWN, she came to see you. This part you're pretty sure of. You remember golden Christmas lights strung cheerily on neighbors' houses when you answered the door. An echo of summer, a flash in your mind: the mosquitoes' golden orbit that first night she came to the screen. Now it was the ugly part of winter. Still so much of the season left to go, still the nights lengthening, snow ice-gritty on the edges of the driveway. You invited her inside, but she wouldn't step off the hallway mat. "My boots," she said. "It takes so long to put them back on."

In a week you would feel it, the hole of her departure. You would finally wrap your mind around it and it would eviscerate you, blow you open like a can on a ledge, clean shot to the outfield, a connection you'd been missing for years and years and finally she would do it, this empty feeling that said: *There*. But in the moment, you just shifted your feet. Kept your gaze on her boots, the time-consuming ones. You couldn't look at her eyes. You kept seeing the way her eyes were in the photograph, half-lidded, sightless as holes. You could almost pretend it was ecstasy that closed them, but even then you knew how to recognize the beauty of something in its violence.

"So I'm leaving," she said finally. "Word got back to my dad about the party. And the picture."

All you could think to say was "Oh."

"They found a school in Arizona that'll take me midyear. You know, fresh start."

Your long silence. Her slow walk toward you, and those boots that left wet prints on the floor. She shoved your chin up with her cold, unmittened hand.

"Look at me," she said.

And you are reminded now, looking out at the falling snow, of how she didn't take her hand away at first. How she held your chin and reached inside her jacket with her other hand, and for a wild heart-stop of a second, you were sure she had a gun, you were sure this was the end.

And then she let you go. You saw the long, black length of what she had pulled from her coat and you recognized the telescope. It felt like a relic from another life. Romy looked down, curled her fingers around the barrel with a tenderness that made you want to back away. Then she looked up.

"I want you to have this," she said. "As, like—you know. A memento. Anyway, I won't have time for it in the dorms." She hesitated. She seemed on the verge of saying something else but didn't. She just stood there and waited for you to take it out of her hands.

And maybe you were about to. God knows you wanted it. Have you ever wanted anything more than the tunnel of her vision, that straight shot to starlight and myth, a route out of your earth-bound body? Maybe one second more and you would have reached out to her, you would have changed everything. But she cleared her throat.

"Also," she said, "thank you. That probably sounds fake, but I mean it. For coming in there. For taking the picture."

You blinked. Things fell out of focus, then zoomed back in.

"Romy," you said, "I didn't take the picture."

"Because it's only when the camera flashed that I woke up. It was so bright, that flash. It froze everything. And then they stopped. I think the flash is what made them stop."

"Romy, I swear, it wasn't me."

"And if you hadn't come in—"

"I *saw* it, but I didn't *take* it."

"Elijah, I'm trying to *tell* you something." Yelling now, and crying a little too, maybe you both were, and you were grateful your parents were out, grateful you wouldn't have to explain all this to anyone but yourself, so horribly, ecstatically grateful you hadn't taken that photograph even though every part of you wished it was yours to take back. Grateful to hear your name out loud, your real name, a name you thought you'd lost—and maybe you did lose it, no one has called you Elijah since. "I'm trying to thank you," Romy said, although her voice was the opposite of grateful. "Thank you for stopping it."

In another world, a cry down the hall. A blanket unswaddled: your best guess. Somewhere deep inside your house, a door opens and softly closes. Outside, the sky dismantles itself with snow, and you can still hear it, the crying in the next room.

You have been waiting your whole life to stop it.

You told her then, one last time, "It wasn't me," and you are almost sure, you would swear anything but your daughter's life on it, that this is true.

"Well," she said. Cast her eyes past you, took the telescope with her. "Then just forget it."

Wedge of Swans

———— ❧ ————

SPRINGTIME IN BOSTON—that first prick of green along the edges of the Common, buds going bulbous on the cleft elms—and what comes out of my palm is a seed. I've been itching for weeks in that long crease in the middle. *The heart line,* my mother used to call it. *Next to the life line.* She would hold my hand and pretend to read it. *This side is the future and this side is the past. And see here, Evie, this empty space, this blank spot in the fold? A fork in the road.*

My mother was an ornithologist. She knew about birds: nesting patterns, mating rituals, how the wingspan of a thrush differs slightly from the wingspan of a robin. She knew nothing about reading palms. She knew nothing, frankly, about humans. Even as a kid, I could recognize that.

But I loved for her to hold my hands, to make them mean something. *Which line is the heart again?* I would ask. *What do you make of this fork in the road?* I understood this meant a choice, but I asked her anyway.

She would laugh, her breath humid and sweet, like red wine and peaches gone soft. A musky, rotting smell. I loved that smell. I don't remember what she said.

Years later, in the golden light of my kitchen, the sun casting sideways shadows through the window and rush-hour traffic pulsing below, I can see that the itchy place in my hand is smack in the middle of that fork. A hole in my heart line, a fault in the canyon of my skin. A little sore has formed there, red and raging from the scratching, an itch so deep inside I don't know if I could get to it even with nails less bitten. I've been trying since my last day of work, and that was three weeks ago. I get a fork from the drawer and dig in with a silver tine, figure maybe that will do it.

Those moments in your life. When you realize you're in the middle of something that has a before and an after. Even then, as I pull out the tine and find the seed sticking to it, bloodied and fragile looking in the sudden light, I recognize that instant for what it is.

A fork in a fork! And I can hear her laugh again, its throaty husk cracking open across time. *A fork in a fork in your life!* The itch still seething, and a deeper ache now too. My mother would have known what to make of it.

THE SEED, ONCE I WIPE IT OFF, is the creamy color of my own skin and so small I would have brushed it off the table had I not seen it come out of me. It looks just like the white millet we used to throw to gather sparrows in the spring. I remember how it felt to sink my fingers deep into the birdseed bag, silky handfuls that became bright-flung clouds above the grass. And then the sparrows' dark arrival, the whole flock swirling in at once, a churning mass, inhuman. I think about that word as I sit at the kitchen table, light wintering back from gold to gray to dark, the pulsing traffic down below slowing like a heart. *Inhuman.* Beside the seed, I feel delicate. I feel otherworldly.

When Josh gets home, I'm still sitting there, and when he flips the light switch, he screams and drops the groceries. I hear his kombucha bottle break inside the bag.

"*Christ,* Evie!" he shrieks. I could be generous and say *yells, cries out, grunts.* But these would be euphemisms. Polite lies. In fact, he shrieks, as quavering and girlish as his scream a moment before. If you want the full truth, he sounds like me when he shrieks, but the version of me I don't like all that much: the one undone by bats and surprises, the gauzy dangle of tiny spiders, the indie slasher films I never want to watch with Josh in the first place. He's been reminding me of me a lot lately. Which would make you think I'd feel more present, not less.

"I'm not feeling well," I tell him finally. My usual line. *I'm not feeling well* is why I haven't changed out of yoga pants in three weeks. Why I spend whole days watching documentaries on C-SPAN and National Geographic. I don't do it when Josh is home, but I think he suspects. He keeps talking about cutting cable.

I look up. Some time has passed. Josh is already cleaning up the broken bottle, the kombucha puddle. The bag is sitting on the counter now, brown bottom softening, and the kitchen smells of vinegar—tart and sweet, like a body at the end of the day.

"You can't keep doing this," he says, though it's unclear what *this* is. Sitting in the dark, maybe. Not finding a job, maybe. "You're going to kill me."

This is ironic. Josh is a paramedic. Technically, so am I. We met in our training program, where he caught my eye across the room during CPR lessons, both of us pumping life into the plastic hearts of our torso dolls. He told me later he liked my rhythm.

"If I kill you," I tell him now, "at least we'd both know what to do." I am trying lightness, a peace offering—it seems only fair—but he doesn't laugh. He's probably tired. He's been moonlighting these past few weekends to cover our rent, and he's always tired, bluish

beneath his blue eyes and generally in need of a shave. I consider
the miracle of that as I watch him from the kitchen table: his need
to shave. The way something grows, day after day, out of the pale
landscape of his cheeks. How impossible that seems, and yet there
they are, these fibers pushing themselves out of his skin, constantly
remaking themselves—the insane beauty of the body, its incessant,
regenerative wonders. I open my mouth to try to say this aloud. But
nothing comes out.

"No, really," Josh says without looking. "Don't get up. Stay there.
I've got it." His voice doesn't sound like mine anymore. It sounds like
my mother's after wine. Some people get blurry with wine, but she
always got sharper.

When he leaves the room, he flicks the switch off. I look down at
my hands, at the table. In the dark, I can still see the seed lying there,
but only if I don't look directly at it.

So okay, I admit: things haven't been good for a while. We aren't
married, but we've been together for four years, and Josh grew up in
Brooklyn. His parents are performance artists, he wears Elvis Costello
glasses and a sand-colored man bun. I understand that being Josh's
partner is the closest thing to marriage we'll ever have. I am fine with
that. My mother is dead, my father never existed. I have no one to
impress with a wedding.

We moved in together almost immediately. A fourth-floor walk-up
in the South End, half a mile from his hospital and half a mile from
mine, in opposite directions. Every morning we walked toward the
lives we would save by walking away from each other. On weekends
we'd read the *Times* in bed, trading sections over an invisible border:
his side, my side. Sex was regular and attentive, a mutual schedule of
exchanges: his turn, my turn. Sundays and holidays, we pulled extra

shifts so we could take vacations to the Outer Banks, to southern Florida and the cliffs of Monterey, all the farthest boundaries of the map we could afford, and in these edge-of-our-lives places we were happy.

And yet: a baby, a baby. Everyone was talking about it, this hypothetical baby. The performance artists when we visited Brooklyn. Our coworkers. My boss, feeling it out during hiring seasons. Josh's hipster friends, who were popping out seconds and thirds and moving away from the city and buying hybrid Highlanders instead of the minivans they secretly wanted. My mom, in my dreams. Josh.

"You're already twenty-nine," he told me. He was younger by two years, that much further from his thirties, and for some reason that needled me more than anything. "Isn't thirty-five the limit? What if we want a few more before then?"

"A few more?"

"Whatever, a couple."

We were in the kitchen peeling peaches, the clingstone kind I hate, the ones that don't release the pit as easily as the kind I grew up with. Josh never knew the right ones to buy at the Haymarket, but he insisted on doing half the shopping, and on doing things like canning peaches in the first place. *Gender parity,* his mother told me once, *is the key to a successful partnership.* Across the room, his father had just nodded.

"My mom had me when she was forty-two," I told him.

"And she was a scientific anomaly. It's a miracle you have no birth defects." His eyes flicked up from his paring knife, then away. "I'm sorry. That was shitty."

It was shitty. But there are things you say and things you tally, and I was too swirly to figure out which this was. Too stuck on the breathless feeling I had anytime we talked about a baby, for reasons I couldn't understand. Of course I wanted a baby. Of course it was logical, the right time, I loved Josh, we would have the lovely little city family he had always envisioned. And yet. That feeling in my chest, scattered and feathery at the edges.

"It's just that we can't afford a baby," I said. "Not now, anyway. Not in this apartment."

My knife slipped past the skin of the peach, right into the edge of my thumb. I swore, and Josh took the peach from me while I sucked on the nick. He peeled it effortlessly, pitted it too, and handed it back to me.

Asshole, I thought.

"We could sell your house," he said, and the feathery feeling took a form, tightened up into a ball inside my stomach. I knew he was right about this, just like I knew the peach he handed me was the same one I'd wanted to eat a second before. But I hated everything about everything right then.

I ate it anyway.

One month later, I told Josh I was pregnant.

MEMORIES, SOMETIMES, OF MY MOTHER:

There is a nest in our backyard, on a low branch at the edge of our property. Two robin's eggs surrounded by tightly braided twigs and other bits of detritus made useful—frayed string and ragged paper, snarls of red hair torn from our brushes and left outside for the birds to repurpose. She lifts me up to look at the eggs, can hold me that high for only a few seconds before she has to put me down, cursing. Lift, glimpse, fall. Lift, glimpse, fall. The eggs are so blue, they glow. They make me think of jelly beans; impossible that something so bright was made by a dull brown robin. I want to hide them in a drawer forever. I want to hold them in my mouth and swallow.

Nature is not made of anything you keep forever, my mother tells me. *Anyway, if you touch them, you'll kill them. You'll leave a human scent, and the mother won't come back.* This makes me want to cry, but I don't because I know she'll stop lifting me. I make her do it a thousand times. When we go inside, I can still feel her hands against my ribs. In the morning I will have two bruises beneath my arms, twin shadows I'll hide from her, my own blue secrets.

AT THE DOCTOR'S OFFICE I learn the sore could be many things. An infected cut. A localized form of eczema. A parasite. Something called Morgellons disease.

"What's that?" I ask.

"Joni Mitchell has it," says the doctor, and I think that sounds nice, glamorous and a little tragic, until he hesitates. "Most doctors understand it to be psychosomatic."

"I'm not crazy." I hold up the birdseed. "This was *inside my hand.* I watched it come out of myself. This is not in my head."

He shrugs. "Morgellons often manifests as both itchiness and the discovery of organic material exuding from the skin. Although usually something more fibrous—strings, growths. Which does not seem to be the case here." I'm not sure why it feels like an insult, a failing on my part to be properly symptomatic, but it does. The doctor looks down at my file instead of me. "It says here you're on Mirena. Any other medications?"

I shake my head.

"And how have you been feeling? Emotionally? Recent changes in family life, employment, sleep patterns?" He is still paging through the folder and won't meet my eyes. I feel tears brinking, threatening to spill. Once, I wanted to be a doctor when I grew up. Then I met a lot of doctors and learned their tricks, the biggest one being that when bad news is coming, they tend to talk to your file and not to your face. Or else they lie.

"No changes," I say, and this too is a lie, but my voice comes out clear and strong and certain. My eyes have sucked the tears back in. Amazing, this body.

"Well, in the absence of additional incidents . . ." He snaps the file shut and smiles. "My best guess is that this was simply a foreign agent."

The phrase makes me think of spies, of duplicitous betrayals. "A foreign agent?"

"Yes. An irritant that entered broken skin and that your body eventually expelled. It can happen long after the initial entry point, of course. Splinters sometimes get lodged for weeks before working their way out. I once removed a small piece of glass from a patient, a teenage girl, that had been stuck in her foot for ten years. The body is like the earth in this way. Eventually it will give up its treasures." He scribbles me a prescription for an antibiotic. "Three times a day. Keep it clean and bandaged. Anything else?"

I'm still hung up on this girl with glass in her foot. I want to ask how they knew it had been there for ten years. Was there a memory so traumatic, something involving broken glass, that she could look back and identify the moment it had gotten stuck? Or does the body have some kind of measurable effect on glass, an erosion that acts like a time stamp, the way the age of fossils can be calculated by compression, or the age of trees by the rings they develop? I want to ask what it was like for the girl to watch that glass come out of her like a hard, sharp miracle, invisible for so long, carried without her knowing. Or maybe she did know, on some down-deep level, and finally here was the proof, the physical evidence of what she had long suspected: *Something is broken inside me.*

I want to ask if he is lying. If this is just a convenient fiction to model a truth about the body.

But I don't. "A foreign agent," I repeat, and leave.

All day long—through the subway ride home, the rain-soaked walk to our empty apartment, the documentary on pelicans I look at but don't watch—I keep hearing that phrase in my head. I hear it loudest when I stare at the bandage in my palm. *A foreign agent.* A carrier of secrets, an imposter. Opaque, impervious, the opposite of glass.

HERE ARE THREE LIES that Josh believes: We have been trying to get pregnant for a year. I had an early miscarriage. We may have infertility problems.

This is the truth: there is a foreign agent in my uterus. An IUD that I asked a different doctor to insert a year ago. I paid cash. "Your insurance will probably cover this," the doctor told me, and I nodded and paid cash anyway. On the way home, I bought the largest, darkest coffee I could find, so strong it made my stomach feel singed. Before Josh got back from work, I had another, weaker this time, but still a second cup when I hadn't had any coffee in a month. ("Abstaining from caffeine is a good way to prepare for conception," Josh said. "I read it online.") The coffee made me jittery all the way to bedtime, to Josh's hopeful hands on me. *You're shaking like a bird,* he said, and I didn't have the heart to tell him it might have been caffeine but might also have been joy. I couldn't tell him why I felt like his body inside me was the freeing, exultant thing it was always supposed to be but hadn't been for a long time.

IN THE MORNING, when I take off the bandage, the sore is still there. Inside the sore is a pebble.

I realize as I'm looking at it, bloodied and hard and almost perfectly round, that I'm not surprised to find it there, which surprises me. I also realize I'm not upset to find it there, which surprises me more. This too-symmetrical thing from nature, unnaturally round, an almost-perfect sphere. This anomaly inside my body, larger and more frank than anything before it: thrilling. A twist to a day that would otherwise have been the same, the same, the same.

I fish the pebble out with tweezers and take a closer look. Creamy white with grayish veins. It reminds me of the larger bony bits in my mother's ashes, which I did not expect to be so substantial when the cremation specialist handed them over in a clear plastic bag. Certainly nothing scatterable, nothing capable of flight: more like coarse sand. Heavier than I thought they should be.

Carefully, I wrap the pebble in a cotton ball and nest it in the bottom of an old white pill bottle. I take the seed from my coin purse and add that too. Looking down at them together in the shadowy bottom, bits of detritus starting to add up to something whole, I think: *a nest in a nest*. The phrase plays over and over in my mind, like *fork in a fork*. Like *foreign agent. Inhuman*.

I don't tell Josh. I don't know why, except that there's a magic in this that feels delicate and only mine. I'm not yet ready to let it loose in the world.

STORIES, SOMETIMES, OF MY FATHER:

He was a hazel-eyed raptor, a bird of prey that stole into my mother's bedroom and clawed her heart, ransacked her life to shreds. Before he flew away forever, he left a tiny egg on her dresser. She watched it for weeks, certain it was a trick. And sure enough, when the egg cracked, out I came with sharp claws and a razor beak like his, ready to attack. But she took me to bed and trimmed down my nails and taught me the habits of the human world, and in this way, she saved me from the fate of raptors, which is to be forever lonely above the earth. In this way, she said, I became hers.

Sometimes my father was a swan, and my mother was Leda, and I was what materialized from that snarl of feathers and fighting: Helen of Troy, precious and powerful. Dangerously beautiful, slaughterer of cities and hearts. *The beauty of the natural world,* my mother liked to say, *is never disentangled from its destruction.*

Sometimes my father was a phoenix, a man who loved my mother with so much fire and passion that it ate him up, left only ashes behind.

And sometimes he never existed at all. That tended to happen during dinner preparation, at the end of a long day at the university that still hadn't given her tenure. Also toward the end of the month. *There are birds that switch sexes,* she would say, chopping onions or furled knuckles of garlic or discount chuck roast. *There are hens who lay a clutch of eggs and later become the cock that protects them. It has to do with the ovaries. A biological mechanism that allows a female to take on the traits of a male if survival demands it.* Usually a full bottle in by now, maybe already on the second, and I would blame my tears on the onions, which never seemed to bother her. *Because what did Adam ever do for Eve? Left her a fucking bone.* I remember the way she wiped the garlic from the blade with her bare fingers. That chill in my spine, waiting for a cut that never came. *You don't need a father,* she said. *The only thing you've ever needed, the only thing you'll ever need, is me.*

AT DINNER, I tell Josh that Dr. Hammond had to push back the infertility appointment. This is another lie that Josh believes.

"Again?" He sighs. "That's the second time. How long?"

"Six weeks. But they say he's the best," I add quickly. "And he's in your network. You know we can't go out of network for this."

My eyelid is doing that twitching thing, that thing that happens when I'm stuck in a lie that is getting too big for me. But Josh doesn't notice. He is pushing his fork slowly across his plate, making patterns in the sauce. We are eating lentils and brown rice. For each other's sake, we pretend it's for the fiber, but I saw Josh cutting coupons for lentils on Sunday. I have turned him into a man who cuts coupons.

He draws a shaky breath and takes my hand, which I pull away—too quickly, I realize, when he looks up. But I don't want him to ask about the bandage.

"How are you doing with this?" he asks quietly.

"With what?"

"Everything." And I realize he thinks it's all wrapped up together: the yoga pants, the darkened living room, the nature documentaries. The uncalled interviewers, the untenanted womb. He pictures me lamenting secretly, alone, that my body is not able to do what we want it to do. I let him think this. It's a logical explanation for something I have no explanation for.

"We'll keep trying the old-fashioned way," I tell him brightly, nudging his knee under the table. "Some guys would be psyched with that plan."

Josh does not seem psyched.

"We could take a vacation," I add. "Somewhere cheap."

He looks at me for a long time. There is a thing in his eyes that goes unsaid. Then he smiles. "I've got some PTO," he says finally. "I could look into flights."

"Somewhere warm."

"Orlando, maybe. The Carolinas. I'll look for promotions."

"Perfect."

"And then we can come back and you can find a new job. It'll be like a reset button. A blank slate."

I rub his hand. I smile with closed lips. "Exactly," I tell him. The ticking in my eyelid like a clock.

FOR A WEEK, I learn about canyons. It's canyon week on National Geographic, apparently. Like shark week, but nerdier. Show after show about the earth and its broken places, its ways of separating.

I tell Josh, "The Grand Canyon is over a mile deep."

"I found a promotion on Delta," he tells me.

"If you fell over the edge, it would take exactly thirty seconds for you to hit bottom."

"Unless you have any interviews lined up, I'll book tickets tonight."

It occurs to me that we are like landmasses, sliding past each other, unlistening. A cavernous space between us.

"There are these base jumpers," I start to say, "who put on winged suits and illegally leap into—"

"Evie, stop." He turns off the television and sits in front of me on the coffee table. "Please. Listen to me. Please *talk* to me."

"We're talking!" I raise my hands. "I'm sorry. Tell me. Vacation."

He smiles. "To Houston," he says. "Next week. Direct flights, crazy cheap. Plus a last-minute hotel deal on South Padre Island. It's only a four-hour drive from the airport, all along the coast."

I just stare at him, my palm itching like mad. "Texas?"

"I know what you're thinking," he says quickly. "And sure, maybe we could tie up some loose ends with the house while we're down there—"

"Loose ends?"

"But a *vacation,* Evie, the whole deal. Cabanas and Jacuzzis and the ocean. I mean, a beach vacation at this price . . ."

He stops. The room falls silent, the television black. The grandness of canyons has contracted to this narrow point of time, this tiny, empty space.

Loose ends, I think, and I picture my little white bottle. The seed, the pebble, and this morning's new addition: a downy curl of reddish skin from a peeled peach. It came out of my sore balled up tight but gradually unfurled once I put it in the pill bottle, like something coming back to life. I thought of the way my mother peeled peaches in one careful, unbroken swirl. What had been round in her hands becoming long and lyrical and alive, spooling slowly across the table like a ribbon, me at one end and my mother on the other.

I tell him, "Book the tickets," and when I go to bed, he doesn't follow.

WHAT IS IN TEXAS:

The wooden floorboards that squeaked in two places when I ran to my mother's room after a bad dream. The first squeak like a baby bird, just outside my door. The second squeak like a mother bird, just outside hers. Call and response, she would say, and although she always sent me back to my own bed, it was the ritual that would calm me. A call, a response.

Also: peach trees. The freestone kind, pits loose and easy, and blossoms that smelled like love itself—honeyed and sweet as my mother's hand soap, as Texas sunsets, watercolor blurry. Every trite thing I once believed in is in Texas.

On the other hand: the X-rays of her bones, stacked somewhere in a doctor's office in Houston. Probably filed in boxes by now, perhaps destroyed. (What do they do with X-rays when the relevant bones are gone? Do they burn them, the way we burn the bodies? Is there a residue somewhere, slick and invisible, of my mother's photographed interior, a transparent melt of plastic lining the inside of some dark incinerator?) Perhaps, in Texas, they are still there, sandwiched together in order. If you held them up to the light in a pile, the skeleton would shine through, grayish and blurry. If you thumbed the pile fast like a flip-book, you could animate the bones, watch them slowly darken as the cancer eats the marrow.

Also in Texas: my mother's will, gifting me an empty house that hasn't sold.

The birds too, all of them. The ones my mother watched from our screened-in porch, the water birds in summer, the migratory song-birds in winter, always a new species arriving, always another leaving. When I went away to boarding school, she would call me in Boston and hold the phone in the air and make me guess the birds by their calls, warbles and trills that spiraled their way through the phone cord in my hand. We would laugh through the static at the names of the flocks: gaggles of geese, charms of hummingbirds, murmurations of starlings. Falls of woodcocks. Dark tidings of magpies.

A LIE THAT JOSH BELIEVES: the house won't sell because the market sucks.

This is the truth: the house won't sell because I haven't tried to sell it.

ON THE EARLY-MORNING PLANE TO TEXAS, Josh holds my hand. He seems giddy and nervous, orders sparkling water in champagne glasses and gets a side-eye from the flight attendant, who reminds us that glass is considered a deadly weapon now. So we toast with the cans. "To a much-needed vacation," Josh says, kissing me hard, and the bubbles are all lightness and heat in my mouth and I can admit, finally, that this was a good idea. We are flying forward into empty space, a blank slate, a canyon of possibility in the palm of our lives together. Anything could happen. Outside the windows the day is splitting open with pale pink light, like a bud, like a tiny seed, growing.

These are the things I have grown in my palm this week:

A sliver of glass.

A knot of blue yarn.

A baby tooth.

A bruise.

Each morning, when I peel off the bandage, a feeling bubbles up in me like Christmas, that sense of a gift waiting to be opened. Or maybe, more accurately, it feels like Advent, like that little wooden calendar my mother set out each year. How it felt when she remembered to fill it with treasures, one behind the door to each day: a chocolate, a pretty shell, a plastic ring.

Today: a bit of bone.

"We're beginning our descent into Houston," the pilot says, and Josh and I slide away our tray tables. We lean into each other a little too hard. "I am so glad," Josh says, looking down at me, and stops. I can tell it's the first half of something, and I wait for the rest. But he just smiles. "I am so glad," he says again, looking right into my eyes. I remember then why I fell in love with him in the first place: that optimism, his boundless faith in the good world, so trusting and sincere it feels like an open wound in danger of infection. I squeeze his hand and try to tell him things with my right palm that I don't know how to say out loud, have never known how to say. I keep my left closed tightly around itself. I can feel something forming there, something made only by me.

THE MIRACLES OF THE BODY:

Nails that can cut, scratch, send shivers up your skin like ghosts, nails that keep growing forward even after all the other parts of you have switched course.

Fingerprints and their little swirls of self.

Whiskers. Soft, then rough, then soft again.

The two-way windows of your eyes.

Ovaries and their tiny clutches of eggs, their furled fists of possibility.

Bones that break, then become unbroken.

Babies. Pinpricks of light growing outward like stars, whole universes of life inside another.

And smaller miracles: the tiny factories of cells and their neat assembly lines, making and making and making. Their microscopic sets of instructions, reams of data—can you forgive a typo here and there? Still a marvel, even when the line breaks down, starts churning out the wrong kind of cell. And the sci-fi plot twist when that new cell sits up, zombie-like, walks off the belt, and takes over the factory—guns down the guys in charge, holds the others hostage—and why stop at the factory when the whole city is there to take over, the world, the metastatic universe? Isn't this too a terrible miracle, a blockbuster story? The way the thing you have made yourself, with your own body, can unmake you in return?

My seed, my knot, my bit of bone: in comparison, they are the smallest of mysteries. The most easily believed, really, among all the beautiful improbabilities.

WE RENT A CONVERTIBLE because we're feeling extravagant. We've saved money by vacationing in Texas, Josh says; we can splurge here and there. On the freeway to the island, we drive too fast, catch the whipping air in our cupped hands. We buy iced coffees at a drive-through, and for once Josh doesn't suggest that I order decaf.

Later we stop at a roadside taquería that sells beers, and I order one, and Josh still doesn't say anything, and that's when I know something really is changing.

At a picnic table, we listen to the traffic buzz past. We watch the gulls swoop, euphoric with sun, and the endless ocean beneath them, deep and blue as a held sigh. The world is so full of itself, so oblivious of any danger. Josh smiles at me and eats his taco and says, "The weatherman said an early summer," and I have never been so aware of the narrowness of the space between happiness and loss. They are two halves, I am realizing, of the same mass, sliding by each other in the night. And love, the canyon in between.

A LIE THAT JOSH BELIEVES but does not ever admit he believes, works actively against believing, imagines he can reverse, pretends does not exist: I don't want children.

This is the truth: maybe I do. Maybe I could love a child. There's that vision of downy skin inside my belly, the closed eyes, the fingers reaching, an imagined knock at my body—there? there?—and then the certainty, the unavoidable awe. The release into the beautiful world. The milk. The tiny cotton socks. The sleepless nights, the clear and urgent and socially acceptable reason for sleeplessness. The way their faces are their own and also not their own, the way others return in the faces of our children: my mother's face. Mine.

And yet. The panic. The sitting up in bed. The listening for breathing beside you, the explosion of wakefulness until you hear it rattling, still there, still alive, still alive?, still alive. The picturing the world without them, the feral scrabble of that thought, the clawed-open gash of it. The tenderness of bones, the sourness of breath, the traitorous body, always growing away from you, and the threats you don't see until it's too late, once nature has come back to reclaim what it handed you, a selfish gift-giver, betrayer of the very heart it made.

I would give anything for something to keep forever.

I would give anything for someone to never leave me.

MEMORIES, SOMETIMES, that are not quite lies but that I have not told Josh, that I can never tell Josh:

For two weeks after my mother died, I lived alone in her house. My house. I was two weeks shy of eighteen years old. The bills had been paid; she'd seen to that. I had a bank account, modest but enough, and a boarding school waiting for me to return from my leave of absence. Still, I kept expecting someone to knock at the door. To send me to foster care or government offices or more doctors or more lawyers—the places to which I could be sent seemed innumerable, impossible—so I locked the door and unplugged the phone.

I wanted no one to touch me.

I wore her slippers, crushed at the heels and molded to her feet. I walked and walked around the house in them, up and down the stairs, in the small circle from kitchen to dining room to living room. The instep didn't match mine at first—I could feel the spaces of her foot, its different shape, the ghost of her skin against my skin—and then, eventually, it did.

I wore her blue cotton sweater, oversized and unwashed, for two weeks. Pale like the sky just before morning. An in-between time, the only time I could sleep. The sweater smelled like her until it smelled like me.

I knew I was waiting for something. It was shaped like the number 18. The shape was *adulthood*. The shape was *then I will know what to do*. The shape was the strong back of a 1, the firm slash of it, lonely and dangerously capable, next to the soft circles of an 8, twinned and curved like two eggs in a nest.

I opened her bottles of pills, and I closed them. I opened them, and I closed them. She had left me enough. It made me wonder.

Small circles. Kitchen to dining room to living room.

I waited for two weeks, and no one came, and then I was an adult. I locked the door when I left. I went back to school in Boston and stayed for its hospitals, where eventually I learned to fix bodies. I met Josh. We saved some lives together, and some others we did not.

WE FINISH OUR TACOS. We order more until we ache with fullness. The beer feels like velvet at the edges of my brain, and the sky is afternoon bright, the clouds pale wisps against the emptiness.

"When I was younger," I tell Josh, looking out at the gulls and their endless loops, "my mother and I would play this game after dinner, naming the flocks of birds. She knew all the names, every scientific term. A wisp of snipes. A watch of nightingales."

Josh is staring at me, motionless, as if he doesn't want to startle the small animal emerging in front of him: I rarely talk about my mother. I don't feel like I'm doing it even now. I feel like these words are coming out of me without my doing anything, without my being aware of their presence until they've formed themselves, surprising and tender and somehow independent of me, loosely knitted, as fragile as bones.

"She would make me guess what was true," I tell him. "That was the game. She would give me the phrase, and I would tell her if it was real or made up. For instance: a knot of wrens. False. A murder of crows. True."

Some time passes. Josh clears his throat. "Didn't you just learn them all eventually?"

"Impossible. There are a hundred names, maybe more. A name for every flock."

He just keeps staring, and I can't look back at him.

"Or maybe I did learn them," I add. "Maybe I just pretended not to know for her sake."

After a while we stand to leave. We throw our glass bottles away, gently, so they don't break in the plastic-lined garbage. On the highway, Josh drives slower, as if even the convertible is sluggish from lunch, or cautious. I sneak glances at him, watch the wind whip his hair around his face, the wild beauty of moving forward, of being alive, and it's a sadder beauty this time, more nostalgic somehow. Even right here in the moment, preemptively nostalgic, as though something about it has already been lost. If anyone deserves truth in this world, it is him.

"A parliament of owls," I tell him suddenly, and he looks over at me.

"It sounds *too* perfect," he says. "Those wise old owls. But I say true. Am I right?"

I smile. His hands on the wheel are steady and sure. The wind in our hair, swirling around our faces, is sucking the birds, one by one, out of my mouth.

"A skein of geese."

"True."

"A host of sparrows."

"True."

"A siege of bitterns."

"Oh, definitely true."

Signs to South Padre now. Exits. So close to arriving.

"Descent of woodpeckers."

"True."

"Unkindness of ravens."

He hesitates, looks over. I can hear it in my throat.

"Deceit of lapwings," I say. "True. Cast of hawks. True. Pitying of doves."

There are tears on my face. They are coming from a body that doesn't seem to be mine. He's pulling over to the shoulder, and the traffic is rushing by us now, the world still moving forward, the world will never quit its moving forward. *Evie, stop,* he is saying, but I can't stop, I can't breathe, I can take nothing in, it all just keeps coming out of me, and all of it is true.

THE FINAL LIE THAT JOSH BELIEVES: there were layoffs at my hospital.

This is the truth: I quit. The day before our appointment with Dr. Hammond, which I later rescheduled anyway, but then, that appointment was a blinding light at the end of the tunnel of my life, a speeding train. I hadn't slept well in days. I dreamt of babies, bombs, nothing left but ashes, I was jumpy on too much coffee and the world glittered brightly just beyond the edges of my vision.

Last ambulance call of the day. It was a girl on Albany Street, a cutter. Underage, drunk, prep-school plaid. Little lines up and down her left arm like a tally, a train track from her hand to her heart. We got the call after she cut too deep and her friends freaked out, dialed 911, split before we arrived; I guess they were scared. But she wasn't, this girl. She was heady and pissed and cursing her friends, cursing the paramedics, fighting us with her thin, bare arms when we loaded her into the ambulance. Eyes so dark I couldn't tell how dilated she was, and skin glowing like a corpse. She was lighter than she should have been. I thought of birds, their empty bones.

In the back of the ambulance I cleaned her arm and checked her vitals. I held her hand at the end of that neat row of tally marks. Thirty of them, maybe more. Some were white, old, almost invisible. You'd miss them if not for the pattern. Others were pink and angry. They reminded me of Lilith, a girl I knew once in boarding school, who used to say she heard voices. She'd had scars just like this, little orderly ghosts in a row.

"Those are mine," said the girl in the ambulance, pulling back her arm. She was calmer now, but in a way that seemed more threatening. Later, when the doctor would tell me about a girl with glass in her foot, this girl's face would come to me: delicate and dangerous.

"How old are you?" I asked.

"Eighteen." Her voice was lacy with phlegm, lips pink and cracked like a porcelain figurine. Blond hair tangled and impossibly fine. Even the ugly parts of her were beautiful.

I stared at her long enough to tell her I knew eighteen was a lie. "Listen, I've been there," I said finally. I'm not sure what I meant by it. The words just came out, and they sounded as empty as I guess they were. She rolled her eyes. "It's not going to help," I added. "The cutting."

"Help what?"

A headache edged my temples, a sense of losing patience. I thought of my mother in her hospital bed. Those last days. The way the ache had sunk so deep into her bones that nothing could touch it, not morphine, not compresses or the heat of my hands. I remembered Lilith curled in a heap on her dorm bed, her palms pressed against her ears. The way the body traps us, I wanted to say. There is no release valve, no easy opening. Only the tacit agreement that you will stay with this body until it is ready to leave you. To damage it—to open it up, on purpose, to pain—seemed so arrogant that I hated her, this girl I'd never met before, would never meet again. I hated how pointless I suddenly recognized my job to be, my attempts to mend people, save them, stitch them, this futile fiddling with clocks that kept ticking relentlessly toward the end.

"It won't get the pain out," I said, and she just started laughing. It wasn't a girl's laugh. It was dark and husky; it smelled like peaches and wine. It unskeined itself from her throat and tangled in me like a knot and yanked something open in my stomach. I would hear it the rest of the day, hear it often over the next few weeks when I sat on the sofa in the dark at a fork in my life, waiting for something to change.

"You people never understand," she said, closing her eyes. "I don't do it to get at the *pain*. I do it to get at the *joy*."

LATER, IN BED, I tell Josh, "A dissimulation." We've undressed in our cheap hotel on South Padre Island. We've had sex with the windows open, the salt air sticky on our skin. Not because either of us wanted to. But it felt like a ritual worth performing, a call and response both futile and necessary.

"What did you say?" he murmurs. His voice is thick. He is almost asleep, my head on his chest. I imagine the flutter of his heart beneath my cheek, something I don't feel but could pretend to feel. I imagine the way we might look from above, all my red hair gunshotting across his skin, a wound we can't see from this angle.

"Dissimulation of birds," I tell him. "That one is true."

"But what kind of birds? A dissimulation of what?" he says. Then he falls asleep.

I lie there for a while and think of my mother, who would appreciate the paradox: dissimulation, true. Who would laugh, probably, at Josh, who does not understand that this is the broadest term for all flocks, that it applies to all birds, to any flock at all—the ravens and bitterns, the falls and dark tidings. The sparrows. Arrivals. Departures. *Dissimulation* is the way Josh's shirt smells when I slip out of bed and put it on, a smell like him, and like home. It's the bathroom's unforgiving white light and the black gummy edge of the bandage on my hand, tattered from tacos and beer and sex. It's finding what I suspected would be underneath, nestled in the crevice of my still-raw sore: a tiny feather, bloody and matted, but downy once it dries. Soft as new pink skin.

Dissimulation is the last loose end, inhuman, foreign, mine. It's the feather I tuck into my pill bottle; it's not waking Josh when I walk out the door.

NOTHING ELSE LIKE IT—the roar of a highway in the Texas dark. Roof down, throat open, sky a black mouth hollering. I can't separate my voice from the world, my own edgelessness from the edge. When I round corners, the rumble strips thunder back: warning signs.

Signs for Houston. I remember the fluorescent buzz of its hospital lights, the wail of babies. Oncology was full, so my mother got the last bed in Maternity, and neither of us could sleep—that constant, seamless screaming of babies through the walls. I watched her toss and turn all night, racked with twitchy pain that snarled the tubes tethering her to food and breath. I'd been born in this same hospital, and in the restless dark, I tried to imagine my tiny body curled and tethered inside hers, waiting to emerge.

At some point she opened her eyes and stared at me without blinking. *Liar,* she whispered, though I hadn't said a thing.

She talked a lot about lies in those last days: the doctors and their myths, their false optimism proven wrong. She was bitter. She had always been bitter, but without her bottles and her birds and even one shred of dignity left to thin it out, the bitterness was unmasked, pungent.

A myth: magpies. Little hoarders. Keepers of pretty, shiny things. When in fact, magpies do not steal shiny things, do not save them in their nests. Magpies are afraid of shiny things, which have no place in nature.

Her voice was ragged. Her hair was gone. She had worn wigs for a while because she was vain, handkerchiefs when she stopped being vain. At the end, she wore nothing at all, and her head was shiny and perfectly round against the pillow, the bluish hue of skim milk.

Swans. Another myth. They don't mate for life. And no lovely song saved for the deathbed. Swans grunt, they hiss and bite and fuck and leave. They are lonely, nasty bastards their whole damn lives.

Did she tell me this then, in the sleeplessness of that last maternity room? Or am I misplacing the memory, a sliver broken off another bedtime story? Once, her myths were about birth and beauty—Leda, Helen. But every pretty thing falls away, and then it's just the shard of truth underneath: lonely girl, nasty-bastard girl, the sort of girl even the nurses would stop trying to comfort. Shatterable girl. Girl who'd push everyone away, every kindhearted consoler, every friend who flew to Texas to visit the hospital, every future lover. Even now I can't help wondering if I ever fully left that last room. If there might be a splinter of me stuck somewhere in Houston, tucked into some unnoticed hospital crevice, still working its way out.

Also, robins. This notion that their blue eggs are camouflage, that it's harder for predators to see a blue egg in the shadows of a nest. Bullshit. The eggs are blue because of bile in the blood.

I remember this curve, this long lean in the road.

The bluer the egg, the more antimutagenic the blood, and the healthier the baby.

My body making the turns without thought, as if it knows what to do instinctively. As if it isn't even mine.

And so the blue egg creates a cycle. Natural selection. The healthier babies—the babies with brighter eggs—get more attention from the mother bird. More food, more nourishment, so those are the ones that thrive, that go on to have their own bright blue eggs. The weaker ones die.

Breathless now, passing headlights scything their silver through me. We are almost there, and I can see how it will go because it has already happened: I will park the car in its spot at the edge of the yard as I have parked the car before. I will walk to the door alone as I have walked alone before. The key will fit like a key always fits—unchanging, permanent. Impossibly shiny. Like nothing in nature.

I will step into the shoes of then and it will be now.

The myth of the robin's egg is that the egg is camouflage, a way to hide. But really, the blue is all about being seen. The blue is a signal to the mother: I am here. *The best chance of survival. Which masquerades, so often, as beauty.*

Would she have closed her eyes, at least briefly, at the thought? She was bitter, sure. But who is immune to the way life can grab you by the throat and remind you that you're here?

And I am. The chatter of gravel stifling to dirt, and then the shush of the overgrown grass, slow roll to a stop, the husk of the house exactly as I left it.

In a moment, daybreak.

In a moment, I will open the door and walk inside and find every emptiness I left there. The flattened sage-green blanket on her bed. The hearth and its unfilled photo frames. The unread books in boxes, the clinking secrets in cabinets, the socks still nestled in pairs, in drawers, the boots lined up in closets, walking nowhere. The table, filmed with a dust made from leaves and dirt and skin and time, all the little bits of the world that have entered through open spaces, all the bits of us the house has not yet released.

I will touch it. I will press myself into it, run my hands across all of it, through the dust and dirt and deep, cottony shadows. I will make tracks in this place to which she will never return, mark each thing with my human scent. I will take it all in, leave nothing unfelt: the taps in the bathroom, the plates, the knives, the wine-dark grain of the cutting board, I will slide my fingers over every cup, my tongue across every spoon. I will open the glaring eye of the bathroom mirror and there will be the bottles, filled with pills gone stale and pointless, and I will add my own little bottle to the neat row and close the mirror and look into myself, my own eyes, my own miraculous body before me—

And then I will leave. Already, I know this. An inescapable truth, like the inner compass that guides the wintering birds back home. I will call the Realtor, call Josh, press the pedal back into the blank space of our lives. But this, I know, is just as true: I will fling this house's windows out to sky before I go, crack it open to the bright blue day. I will let the dust fly up, an exaltation of dazzling light.

I turn off the car. Time holds still for a moment, engine ticking, morning coming into color. Larks are unfurling their throats into song. My hand aches. I think of that fold in my skin and what might have formed it, that fork I've been moving toward my whole life, both knowing and not knowing it was there. Was it something I held when I was young, some imprint? A certain way I closed my fist? Or does it go back even further, back to the beginning, to her, the pinprick of me floating once in empty space? Does it go back to that first moment I stretched out my hand to touch the world I thought was mine, a world that belonged, that whole time, to someone else?

Helen in Texarkana

———— ❧ ————

CLAIRE HAS BEEN dreaming of crows. Shiny black rumbles in the back of her brain. Dark feathers twitching against her skull. They've been keening every night outside her bedroom window, the same rhythmic caw again and again, and she's beginning to think she almost understands it, their guttural, back-of-the-mouth language. Sometimes she rolls it in her own mouth just to have a say in the matter—quietly, into her pillow, so she doesn't wake the baby. The words feel foreign and sticky. *Caw*. Like toffee on her tongue. She wants to suck on the sounds, hard enough to hurt them.

Dark, winging thoughts. Not the thoughts of a mother, she thinks, then unthinks it.

Meanwhile, the baby is speaking French again. This is the third time in a month. When it first happened, Claire thought it was a fluke—a funny story, one to share with her husband over dinner. "À demain," the baby kept calling from her crib. "À demain, à demain," pointing her chubby fingers toward the window. Claire remembered the phrase from eighth-grade Intro to French: *à demain, see you tomorrow.*

But in the mouth of her one-year-old, it sounded so close to *animal,*
animal that Claire thought the baby was just pointing at the crows.
They had already begun to cluster in the neighborhood, though
spring was still raw then, had scarcely cracked the ice.

At dinner all her husband said was, "Now you're putting words
in her mouth too?"

The baby loved the crows. Back then, even Claire could muster
up an appreciation: if nothing else, they carried with them an eerie
beauty. On the power lines, they settled and grew still, folded their
wings, spaced themselves evenly in rows like bright black pearls.
Claire would hold the baby and together they would press their hands
against the window glass, point and echo each other's words. *Crow,*
animal, yes, fly away, yes. Their fingerprints left gauzy patterns, poin-
tillist blurs that reminded Claire of the paintings she had made once,
before her studio became a nursery. She was often tempted to leave
them there, these ghost-hands marking the glass like small, breathy
spirits pressing in from the outside. But her husband polished them
away, and after a while the crows migrated from the power lines to
the roof, where their talons scuttle and tap invisibly: dashes and dots,
a code she can't interpret.

The town has sent notices. We are aware of the issue; the crows
are attracted to vermin; this street has not adhered to county waste-
management protocols; are you sure you haven't brought this on
yourself?

Claire is not sure. Most things feel like she has brought them
on herself without knowing exactly how. The emptiness in her bed.
The craggy scar on her stomach. The baby chips a tooth (a stumble,
a chair leg) and she feels the neighbors side-eyeing her at the swing
set, looking for bruises, thinking: *What kind of a mother.* The baby's
head is scabby with cradle cap, molting dandruff that glows in her
dark brown fuzz, and every person Claire meets knows just what she's

doing wrong—the nannies at library circle, the grocery bagger, even the crusty grandmother with dementia at the park—all of them full of wisdom and correction. Use this oil, leave it alone, comb it out, rub it in, give it time, don't wait, time is of the essence. She remembers strangers' hands reaching out to touch her round belly: the sudden claim the world had to her body, a body that had become alien to her.

Even the French—this is another fluency she lacks, which embarrasses her, since she was an artist (perhaps, in her finest moments, an intellectual) before she was a mother. Her husband, a professor of ancient Greek, has no such lack. He can translate six languages and has published in all of them. In the hospital he spent most of Claire's labor exchanging French jokes—which went literally over Claire's head—with the obstetrician, who was from Marseilles; if he wanted to, he could speak French to the baby at will, without hesitation, and with a perfect accent. He may very well have done so in those dark, lost hours before Claire woke from the anesthesia.

Perhaps this is why she finds a secret comfort in this: the baby refuses to speak French to her father, to anyone else. Only to Claire.

The second time it happened was a week ago. The baby was in her high chair eating grapes, whole, chokeable grapes Claire hadn't cut in half because already she could see a certain worn path within the landscape of this new life—always cutting things in half—and it was becoming clear to her that what was at stake was only partially her sanity. It was also about her child becoming a child of the world, a world where any number of dangers lurked around sudden corners (the wall socket's black eye, the hungry mouths of staircases, plastic bags, bottles, boredom, the sudden corners themselves), and how would her daughter survive if she didn't end it somewhere? Didn't stop this trickling down of danger, hidden deaths even in this, a mere grape? Plus her husband had just left her. Plus all the knives were dirty, and who knew if she could wash another knife without cutting something?

So: whole grapes.

It was a fragile morning, spring having recently split Ohio's gray to a tender yellow-green. Sun coming through the window made slippery patterns of light on the kitchen table; the breast milk in the baby's cup would look the same if Claire reached out and spilled it. That's what she was thinking about, light that seemed milky and cruel, when she heard the sound. Guttural, a foreign threat. Like a marble skittering, or a crow. Claire felt something soar into her throat as she looked up (the baby's dark eyes bugging, the clenched fear of her tiny lips), and she was moving before she told herself to move, she was pounding on the baby's back, trying to lift her, all of this without thinking. But the straps were fastened and the buckles were complicated, so Claire lifted the whole thing into her arms instead— the wooden high chair, the baby strapped, the milk flying—and she shook everything upside down until something flew out of the baby's mouth.

Claire expected a grape. It was not a grape. What flew out was a sound: *"Je suis désolé, maman. Je suis désolé."* Claire didn't know the words—she would look them up later—but there was a shape to the sound that was like a shadow, both there and not there, an outlined absence she could recognize.

The baby was crying desperately. Claire put the chair down and unbuckled her, lifted her close. She felt a splintering love. Or maybe, even more deliciously, its aftermath: she felt something coming back together. "It's okay." She said it out loud to the baby, and also to herself. She said it so many times, it lost its meaning. "It's okay, it's okay, it's okay." The baby's breathing slowed, but her wrists stayed clamped around Claire's neck, fingertips cool as pearls. Out the window, Claire could see crows sweeping purple shadows across the yard. Her arm muscles began to shake, a gorgeous ache coming gradually into color as she looked down at the high chair. Antique, a gift from her mother-in-law. Solid wood. Impossible that she had just lifted it, let alone turned it upside down. Impossible that the baby was fine, was in fact laughing now, tickling Claire's neck as if it had all been a game. And yet this was true: she had known exactly what to do, an instinct let loose from inside the cage of her body. She felt the door still swinging.

Little fingers pecking at her skin. Sweet pink voice still babbling: *"Désolé, désolé, désolé."*

SO CLAIRE IS WATCHING FOR IT when it happens for the third time. Almost eager for it, though she dreads it too, an inner jumble that reminds her of the art studio where she met her husband. Back then, she was a tense and wary painter, and she remembers the dark satisfaction of the moment her brush would inevitably slide beyond the borders of the image in her head. A mistake, yes: she understands there is something wrong with a baby who speaks French in Ohio. But also the cool rush of relief. Finally, she could stop anticipating her own failure. Finally, the shapes of her shortcomings would be known.

It happens in the backyard. The baby is playing in the sandbox, poking black feathers into little hills. Claire is walking the perimeter of the house with the exterminator, who is explaining that little can be done. "The thing about crows," he says, nodding at the roof, "is that they're social creatures. Same as people, really. Once you get a group of them together, they're like a family. Hard to disperse."

The exterminator has sinewy brown arms and green eyes that glow in the heat. It's springtime, but the thermometer says ninety, promises higher, and it's been nine days since Claire has spoken to anyone besides the baby. The sun is stretching its golden legs deep into the afternoon. Her mouth feels dry with words, though that may just be last night's whiskey.

"Not all families are hard to disperse," she says.

She watches his eyes skitter down her long brown ponytail, her breasts, her pink blouse. Silk. Unbreathable. Much too hot for this weather. The air is throbbing with the distant calls of crows.

Claire is waiting for him to ask the question she needs to hear out loud: *Where's your husband?* To which she could acknowledge, finally, to someone other than the uncomprehending baby: *On sabbatical in the Berkshires, fucking Gladys, who teaches romance languages and has tremendous, perky, unsuckled breasts.* She wants him to ask. She wants to shock someone.

But the exterminator only looks away. "True," he says, clearing his throat. "In any case, this isn't like getting rid of an anthill. We don't have any chemical remedies. Nothing, really, beyond the traditional. Which means your main options involve fear."

"Fear?" This approach sounds so simple to Claire, so breezy, and at the same time, comically impossible. "You mean scarecrows?"

"Sure, or even just movement. Garden pinwheels on the roof. Strings of fishing line. Any movement will do. You've got to make sure they don't *want* to return."

"I suppose that's always the best way." A crow peeks down at them from the roof with one shiny, unblinking eye. "Passive-aggression."

"Exactly. They're animals. But they're smart animals."

"Animals." She stares at the crow, who stares back, a challenge. *À demain, bitch.*

"Noise can work," says the exterminator. "If you're desperate. I've heard you can record the crows' distress calls. Play the tape on a loop, full volume, to keep them away. But that fix might be worse than the problem."

"Phantom crows," she says.

He laughs. She doesn't. She's lingering on the possibility of harnessing distress. Packing it into a cassette, an object no larger than her hand, and making it useful.

"Will a gun work?" she says.

"Like a shotgun?" He laughs again. "You live in town."

"Well. The neighbors got a gun."

This is mostly true. The gun is Claire's, a snub-nosed Ruger she bought last week after a dream about intruders. But the question stands: she's not clear how effective it would be.

The exterminator looks at her for a long time. His green eyes are a forest. The fairy-tale kind, full of haunting things and plunder. Then he looks at the baby, who waves at him with a gritty hand. "A gun is probably not the best plan," he says slowly. "See, you can't just scatter them. They'll find their way back. They always find their way back to each other."

Claire's throat grows tight with something that wants out. She feels tears brimming and he looks quickly away. The exterminator is polite like that—thoughtful, considerate. He would be a generous lover. When he crouches down next to the baby, who babbles nonsensically at him, he's smiling again. "She's sweet, huh?"

"She likes you. She only throws sand at people she likes."

"I get that a lot." He holds out a hand. The baby touches his finger with her own—two tips connecting, God and Adam—and continues to babble. "I have no idea what she's saying."

"Same," says Claire. "It's all French to me."

"You mean Greek."

"No. French."

The exterminator rises. His body unfolds to a length that twangs deep in her stomach. She can practically feel it in her palms, the heat of his back, his spine stacked against her fists like knobby puzzle pieces—the logic of bones, of their bodies, each chiseled part clicking into place. "Like that Frenchman on the news," he says. "You hear about that? Guy wakes up with amnesia in New Orleans and it turns out he's some French tourist with head trauma. And now he can't speak French anymore, only English. And the thing is, he didn't even *speak* English before."

Had she read this in the paper? It sounds vaguely familiar but only in the way a dream is vaguely familiar. All the separate parts recognizable, but not the story they add up to. "That's incredible," she says.

"Right? Total blank. Can you imagine?"

"I can," she says, and it's true: as he turns to leave, she can feel an old panic reaching across time. The inscrutable, silent canvas in front of her, white as hospital sheets. Brush in her hand and the edgeless possibility of any mark to be made. She presses her palm to the exterminator's shoulder and feels him freeze, feels it all funnel down to a single red point. "Can you?" she says, and together they look down at the baby, who throws her hands high into the air.

"*Oui, allons-y!*" she shouts, scattering sand at their feet. "*Oui, allons-y!*"

CLAIRE MET HER HUSBAND at Kansas State, where her father was an adjunct in agricultural sciences and her future husband an instructor in the Atelier program. The Atelier was a graduate seminar, a multidisciplinary course deconstructing Greek myths through collaborative art. But somehow, on the strength or misreading of one of her paintings, she had been accepted into it—she, a full-ride undergraduate (need-based, not merit), a painting major who still lived at home and worked nights at the saltine factory where her older brother worked days. Her future husband was a classics PhD candidate with round tortoiseshell glasses and the sort of carefully arranged messiness—sandy scruff and tousle, ageless tweed pilfered from another time period—that she knew by then only money could buy.

His glasses were fake. She could tell from across the studio on the first day of class, as he lectured on and on about the differences between Homer's Helen, Virgil's Helen, Ovid's Helen. "The lie of Helen," he said, waving his pencil with abandon, "is that there was ever one Helen of Troy. There are innumerable Helens, *unresolvable* Helens—the whore, the faithful. The traitor, the loyalist. The feminist, the pawn. The object, who was stolen. The subject, who wanted it. And this, of course, is the gift of Helen to the artist: the ability to make her *yours*." With every turn of his head she watched his glasses, the way the light was never distorted, the edge of his face never broken into separate planes: fake glass. She was sure of it. For reasons she couldn't articulate, the glasses infuriated her, rumbled up in her stomach the fact of her scholarship, the vague haze of her post-graduation plans, the imposter feeling she had every time she showed up for his class. The glasses made her think of the smell of crackers and their neat, unbroken, parallel lines when they came down the plane of the belt, a queasy feeling, though she interpreted the lurch as mere desire. He was exceptionally attractive. And she was exceptionally tired, as a college senior, of living at home.

So when he approached her after class one day, all the other paint-flecked artists and tortoiseshell translators filing out of the studio, she was hungry for it: a word, a criticism, anything. Even from him. Especially from him. She had always been an A-minus student, eager to please, effortful and not quite magnificent, but full of the sort of floral promise that made her feel constantly on the verge of being recognized. *A budding talent,* her teachers had said over the years. *A developing eye, a late bloomer, tremendous potential.* She'd been a full-ride kid at boarding school too, and after graduation, when she moved back home for college—the only girl in her class to do so— that feeling hadn't gone away, the sense that everyone was off to their real lives while she remained, eternally, on the cusp of hers. So yes, she was hungry. She wanted her work to be seen through his empty glasses, witnessed with unmitigated clarity. She wanted him to say out loud what was in front of him so she might finally know it herself.

But all he said was, "You're overthinking it."

Claire continued to dig into her palette with the knife, blending, blending, until the ocean blues tamped down to a steely gray. He was standing so close behind her. She could smell his aftershave, a crisp, wooden smell like cedar, and the human tang of his breath that was not entirely unappealing. "Overthinking what?"

"The whole scene. Helen, the ramparts. Your Trojan horse is a *horse,* for God's sake. Remember, the goal of translation, both linguistic and visual, is to get past the literal to the *sense* of a text. Which is to say: your issue here is rationality. Too much head, not enough pulse."

She turned around and held the wet palette knife between them. It was perilously close to the soft brown weft of his tweed jacket, as overt a defense as she could muster with years of midwestern passive-aggression behind her. What she wanted to say was that his words meant nothing to her and she suspected they meant just as little to him. Instead, she said, "You haven't even asked me what it's about."

"What is it about?"

"Imposters. Fakes." She watched his eyes as she said it, but they didn't blink. "The sack of Troy isn't really about Helen. It's about deception. Troy falls because a fraud gets through the gates, a horse that is not really a horse. That's the artistic problem I'm exploring. How do you represent something that everyone knows is a misrepresentation from the start?"

He was starting to smile. His eyes, which were a blackened toffee gold, a burnt palette she couldn't break down into its components, glinted with a joke she didn't understand, and she felt the rumble in her stomach again, but clearer this time: anger.

"Don't laugh at me," she said, and the thrust of her voice surprised her.

"I'm not laughing," he said, laughing. "I'm just . . . pleased. You're starting to think like a translator."

"But I'm not a translator. I'm one of the artists."

"We're all translators. Translating is just moving things from A to B. You're still at point A, which is literal. You're paralyzed by the first image of Helen that comes to your mind because it comes to everyone's mind. That's why your painting looks like every other painting we've discussed, even before you've finished Helen. You aren't considering B."

Claire turned to her canvas. A gray swirl of smoke, the burning city, the muscular bulk of a wooden horse. In the middle a white space yawned, vaguely sketched, an emptiness she was saving for some iteration of Helen's body. She hated to admit it, but it did, in fact, already look familiar, even with nothing there.

"Okay," she said. "What's B?"

He took her hand gently and guided the palette knife toward the canvas, pointing. "We already know this story," he said. "The Trojan horse arrives at the gates. A war gambit, a con job we misread as goodwill. The Greeks are the imposters. We invite them inside and Troy falls. Right?"

"Right."

"But *that's* the misreading. The real fraudulence belongs to Helen. This woman no one has been able to read consistently, that no poet can pin down, this beautiful mystery."

Claire could feel his breath on her neck. Hot ghost on glass, fogging the edges of her attention. She was still technically a virgin, and she had never studied a man's hand so closely in the light: the golden landscape of the skin that covered hers, the fine hairs that quivered like filaments as he scraped her palette knife gently, then not so gently, against the canvas. The friction of metal against gesso jazzed up her spine, and a burning building disappeared beneath a smear of gray. She didn't stop him. She wasn't sure why.

"In Stesichorus," he said, still pressing the knife in her hand to the painting, "Helen never went to Troy at all. The gods split her in half and made two Helens, one real and one an eidolon. A phantom. It was the phantom who went to Troy with Paris, the ghost they all burned for. The Helen we *think* we know, the Helen that has obsessed us for millennia, was never even real. The real Helen was in Egypt the whole time, at home with her husband."

"Doing what?"

"Who cares? No one writes that story. And it's not the point. The point is, as you said, fraudulence. Because Helen of Troy is an empty space, a floating signifier, she can be whatever we want to make her. She can be, for instance, a ghost." He flipped the palette knife over and slid the caked gray paint through the white space of Helen's absent body. "But she might also be a lover, a conspirator." He took Claire's empty hand and pressed it hard against the wet canvas until their prints slid together through the horizon; near and far began to blur, the world shallowing to a flat plane. "And she might also be dangerous. As creative as she is destructive." He wrapped their fingers together around the hilt of the knife. The gray layer of paint between their hands slipped and warmed. "The imposter was always Helen," he said, and he pressed the knife into the canvas and pulled down— they pulled together—until a long slash exposed the pale wooden frame beneath. "This is why we love her and hate her, why we can never resolve her. Because there is no *her* underneath it all."

The room was silent, but Claire could still hear, in its aftermath, the sound of splitting fabric. The laceration gaped like a wound. Later that night, alone in the vague dark of her childhood bedroom, these were the things she thought of as her hands crept down and the memory spiraled to a hot white point, focused and sharp.

The next day Claire's other professor—the one who was actually an artist—was waiting in front of her split canvas, rapt. Brilliant, he said. Visionary. Had she considered next steps, an MFA, perhaps an installation? Across the room, the man who would someday be her husband was watching through his distortionless glasses, silent. When she slept with him a week later, she pretended to know exactly what she was doing, though they both knew the truth.

TEN YEARS LATER, it's the eidolon that Claire remembers as she watches the exterminator drive away in his white van. The way a body can seem substantial one moment, incorporeal the next. How swiftly and efficiently she could make a ghost of the green-eyed man: the warm heft of his back a clear promise beneath her palm, a solidness there for the taking, and just as suddenly—vanished. *Excuse me, ma'am, but I think you might have the wrong idea.* Even adultery a language she can't speak.

It takes some digging, but she finds the Frenchman in an old newspaper from last week. A fortunate consequence of neglecting the recycling: here he is, the man she is looking for, waiting in a dusty corner of the garage. The Frenchman's photograph is made of many tiny gray dots that come together to form a wry, clever face. A familiar face, the face of her husband from long ago, back when he was wry and clever instead of gone. When she touches his mouth, the dots smear against her fingers and blend. When she pulls her hand away, tiny parts of his face stay stuck to her skin. Smudged, the resemblance is even more striking.

Pascal Duval, says the newspaper. Concussion, amnesia, linguistic dissociation due to damage in the frontal lobe. Transferred to University Hospital in Houston, where a doctor specializing in speech and language disorders has been quoted: "Imagine waking up into a life that isn't yours, a fluency to which you have no claim. He is recovering well, given the traumatic circumstances."

This is when the crows start to crash into the windows.

At first, just one thump. Claire hears it from the garage and finds herself running, heart hammering, thump resonating—a thump the same tenor as a baby's head against furniture. But no, here is the baby, stacking blocks and knocking them over again and again, and it takes Claire some time before she sees the body of the crow lying just outside the sliding glass door.

She unlatches it and kneels on the patio. The crow is still twitching, neck wrenched to a startling angle, bluish-black wings heaving. The beak, which is dark but unpolished, a less expensive glisten than the feathers, is long and slightly pointed, and Claire can see a tiny black tongue inside. She feels a strange urge to pull on it. To plumb it with her fingers, follow its path deeper, yank open the glossy throat and discover what callousness resides at the root, what ugly, thunderous heart has been forming the noise that follows her each night to sleep. (She could just as easily slice open from the stomach, she knows. The way her father used to do with Kansas pheasants in the garage before handing her the pretty tail feathers. The way the doctors must have done to her while she was fast asleep. She imagines the drag of the scalpel through flesh, remembers the sound of the palette knife splitting canvas and how as a child she used the pheasant feathers as paintbrushes, all of this coming without any sort of connected logic, like a string of babble from the baby.) But the neighbors might be watching. So she presses her hands against the wings, a gentle touch, one that would appear, from a distance, to be motherly. She waits until the crow's breath slows to match her own breath, the way she waits sometimes for the baby to fall asleep in her arms even though all the books say not to.

She sits there until she is sure. She sits and thinks of the baby stacking blocks behind the glass, an endless piling up just to knock them down and start again. She thinks of Pascal Duval, a face of dots coming together in patterns, and the miniscule gray layer of him that exists between the crow and her fingertips. She thinks, as she stands and looks at the baby through the glass, of her husband. Of floating signifiers. Of nine days. Of the exterminator's iridescent green eyes: *Any movement will do.*

Without thinking—instinctively, like any bird drawn to its own reflection—she begins to pack for Houston.

THE TOWN OF TROY, OHIO, was a joke at first. Something they laughed about during those perfect, glittery years of early marriage— first the elopement from Kansas to Boston, and then the beautiful city unfolding like a fairy tale, its golden dome, its silver buildings and boats made of swans. His postdoc at Harvard. Her first show in Cambridge and that rave review in the *Globe,* the eager call from a South End gallery. Perhaps, in her previous life, she would have noticed them sooner, all the dark doubts winging at the edges. How the reviewer, her husband's Harvard colleague, had flirted with her shamelessly at a department mixer; how the gallery owner, an old family friend of her husband's father, asked to speak with him first. The way their lovely Back Bay apartment, a penthouse loft his trust fund could afford, always made her feel like a very important guest. But for a while, all she could see was the golden skyline, the future that rolled before them like one long, open horizon.

New York next, they agreed. In New York, there was Columbia, SoHo, a city they would plunder together, two stars rising in tandem. And after he got tenure, perhaps some time abroad in London, Paris, Vienna.

"Of course, there's always Ohio," he would joke. A colleague had sent him a posting: tenure-track Greek at a women's college in Day-ton, with affordable housing in nearby Troy. He dismissed it immediately (the real job offers would come, of course, from the research institutions) but laughed about it with her in bed. "You have to admit, there's a certain romance. Troy, the place we began. Troy, the place we could end, looking down at the ramparts of academia. The charred remains of the dreams of better scholars."

"Stop it. You sound like an asshole."

"And you?" He kissed her neck.

"And me?"

"Painting all day in the Midwest. The lush, fertile, verdant Midwest. Helen all night, burning."

"You mean Northeast. Isn't Ohio Northeast?"

"Unequivocally Midwest." His mouth, going southbound, sounded sure of everything. She smiled into the dark, found his hands beneath the sheets.

It was only when the job offers didn't pour in, when the trust fund proved shallower than expected, when the bills began piling up in slippery stacks, that Troy became something other than a joke. A pit stop, he said now. A chance for him to finish his book, to publish and make his name, remap his scholarly path.

"And me?" she asked.

"And you? Think of it like one long artist's colony. A house amid nature. Woods and birds, peace and quiet—people kill for that. And what a place to raise a family. Don't you think?"

"Don't I think what?"

"About family." His eyes flicked just past her shoulder, and she understood in that moment that he was afraid. That perhaps the skyline was big enough for only one of them.

Of course, the college in Dayton loved her husband. A big tweed fish in a tiny pond. And he loved them back for what they offered— time to write, adoration, tenure. The art market of Ohio was precisely what she expected it to be, which is to say: by the time her husband suggested her studio might also become a nursery, she didn't argue, because what was the point.

They bought a lawn mower. A sectional. A multiyear insurance plan as square and safe as Kansas. In the mirror, her pregnant body Picassoed to pieces, rounding here, darkening there, until she couldn't recognize the whole. Until her husband refused to touch her with anything but exquisite, art-object delicacy; refused to slap her, even when she asked.

("Honestly, Claire," he'd say, more surprised than repelled. But still. "You need to start thinking like a mother.")

What he'd never explained—and she told him this one morning in Troy, staring out the kitchen window—is who the eidolon thought she was. Did she know she was a ghost? Or did she think she was real?

"You're being dramatic again," he said.

Perhaps she was. But it seemed a fine moment for drama, her belly a globe by then, a world that shuddered with invisible will, limbs pressing upward in grotesque peaks. At any moment she could be earthquaked right open. He sighed and wrapped his arms around her stomach, and they looked out together at the blank green lawn. "The point is not how she felt," he said, "but how *you* feel about *her*. Romance or tragedy—it's your story to shape, Claire. That's the beauty of translation. Bend it this way and it's a love story. Bend it that way, the whole city burns."

SOUTHBOUND. IN HER LAP, a map to Houston and a hospital room number (1001, a leering palindrome, eye-like), which a cheerful receptionist gave her over the phone. *Oh, Pascal! Such a charmer. Don't tell him I said it, but we're all a bit in love.* Behind Claire, the baby jabbers long soliloquies from her car seat. On either side of the road stretches an indecipherable horizon. Here it is scribbly with overpasses. Here it is dog-eared with cornstalks. The cornstalks bend down and become cotton; the cotton darkens to a field pocked with buzzards. How much time has passed, how many miles? The only certainty is the freeway, cracked gray spine holding the country together.

Sometimes, in the rearview mirror, a feathery fleck of calligraphed black—but gone before she can catch it in focus.

They stop occasionally to stretch and nurse. The baby seems to like road trips. She waves from the backseat and shouts, *"Bonjour, maman!"* at random intervals. She points out the window and yells, *"Avion! Dans le ciel, avion!"* Claire lets her eyes float upward to the vast, empty blue and finds it: a ropy, smoky slash from an airplane so small, she can't even see the thing itself, only the ghost of its passing.

"Ghost," Claire says out loud.

"Fantôme," says the baby.

"Phantom," says Claire.

"Eidolon," says the baby.

She feels the memory unclasp. "That's Greek," she says, eyeing the baby in the rearview. "What are you saying? Did your father tell you to say that?" But the baby just smiles, reaching toward the window for the plane, her sticky hands splayed wide as stars.

(In the gauzy dark of a years-from-now bedroom, when Claire tells her daughter the story of Pascal Duval, this will be the vision that cleaves to it: the baby's hands, so far away from that distant silver body. Her unapologetic, open-fisted way of wanting. It's a small moment in a long journey, certainly less dramatic than the broken glass that happens later, the yard full of dead crows, the thrust of the man who will cry her name over and over as if in pain, all these shatterings still to come. And yet the bit of grit this story will some-day pearl itself around will be those tiny hands, straining to hold the pretty smoke that is nothing more than aftermath. The proof of an invisible presence sliding its shell across the sky.)

When the car breaks down, they're on the outskirts of Texarkana. First a guttural moan from deep beneath the hood, and then a slow roll, a stop. The engine death-rattles steam into the air, which is black and soulless with rural midnight. And lonely. The highway she's stalled on is sparsely traveled, and Claire knows the smart thing now would be to stay in the car, wait for morning, a country traveler, a police cruiser, help. Never leave the vehicle: that's the rule. Of course she knows that. Certainly the smart thing is not to walk along the side of the road, baby sleeping against her shoulder, toward the glints in the distance that look like farmhouse lights but turn out, once she gets closer, to be nothing but street lamps. The smart thing is not to stand there, weighing the options on the shoulder of the highway, until headlights bloom behind her—headlights that could be anyone, with any kind of intention. Headlights that ogle, lustrous, seize her body with glare and press its outline against the dark sky, headlights that wake the baby. The smart thing, of course, is not to wave them down.

And yet—who is this woman stepping into the road? Claire watches her walk toward the light. Hopes she might know what the hell she's doing.

IT TURNS OUT the headlights belong to a trucker—an old man, stern and gray and headed for San Antonio, who leans out of his cab with a leering smile. *"Houston?"* he repeats, hawking the word like tobacco. "Right far 'way this time of night. And you all alone out here. Where's your husband?"

There on the shoulder of the road, the image of Gladys hovers like a country ghost. Her long, thin hands. Her skin like cream in tea, and her husband's apology-that-was-not-an-apology, standing in the door before the screen slapped him away: *I just need to see where this goes, Claire.*

"We're meeting my husband in Houston," Claire says. "He's in the hospital. Doesn't speak the language."

"A foreigner, huh?"

The trucker has a walleye that unnerves her in the moonlight. It makes her feel hazy, as if she's standing just off-center from herself. "He's . . . from Paris. That's where we met."

"Oh, Toto. I don't think we're in Paris anymore." The trucker chuckles, or maybe coughs, an imprecise sound crackling with phlegm. Then he opens the door and holds out a hand. The baby squeezes Claire's blouse into fists of curdled silk. *"Fais de beaux rêves,"* she whispers.

As the trucker drives the last stretch to Houston, the baby murmurs French lullabies in her sleep, and Claire's dreams plunge her home. Her house is empty. Her husband returns. He walks from room to room, taking note of the abandoned mess—scattered blocks, tipsy towers of food-scabbed dishes, dust thick in the crotch of every chair. He is apoplectic. Where has his family gone? He raises his hands to his face, which is made of burlap. He tries to speak, but the shiny black thread on his lips holds tight, his mouth a gash stitched up to silence. And so when the caw of a ringing telephone spirals through the air, loops its music through the long wire hitching the house to faraway Arkansas—or is it Texas by now?—he tries to answer but can't. His hands are made of hay, his throat is filled with sawdust. *Pick up,* she tries to tell him. *Hello? Are you there?* His back is to her and she can't see his face, just the scarecrow slump of his body on the pole, and when he finally turns around, his face is not his face, his face is Pascal Duval's, and she wakes. The sun on the horizon is a single bloodshot eye. "Houston," says the trucker, and the baby wails, hungry for milk.

CLAIRE HAS BEEN TO TEXAS only once before, to stay with a boarding school friend as her mother was dying. The girl, Evie, had asked her to visit during spring break of their senior year. By then, Claire barely knew Evie. They'd been close as first-formers but had drifted so far apart that Claire couldn't fathom why, of all their Briarfield dormmates, she was the one Evie called from Texas. But how could she say no?

And so she'd used her last airline credit to fly to a Houston hospital and watch Evie watch her mother die. That must be the reason, Claire figures, that *this* Houston hospital—which is not the same but feels the same—incites such a strong sense of déjà vu. Perhaps all Houston hospitals use the same interior decorators, she thinks. Or the same generic cleansers: that disinfectant pucker, a smell like turpentine, and beneath it, the tang of bodies unbecoming themselves. Doctors and nurses stare as she walks down the white halls, baby on her hip. As if they know—how do they know?—that she is an imposter. And this too reminds her of spring break with Evie, a trip she realized almost immediately was a mistake. Evie's mother slept the entire week. Evie perched at the end of her hospital bed, braiding and unbraiding her own long hair, and Claire felt hopelessly out of place, never knowing what to say or where to look—anywhere but the newborn baldness of the mother's head. She mostly said nothing. On the last day, when the complications worsened, Claire took a taxi alone to the airport. "I'm so glad you were here," Evie told her in the hall, but her gaze went right through Claire, arms folded in a stance that made clear a hug was unwelcome. Claire didn't attempt one. She said goodbye and flew back to Briarfield and regretted that not-hug the whole way home.

Claire hasn't thought of Evie in years. And what comes back now is less the specific memory of Evie than what Claire felt like in that hospital room, somehow both invisible and conspicuously fraudulent.

Like the exterminator flinching away from her hand—how he looked at her then, a wary squint, as if he could no longer see her clearly. Like the doctors who gawk at the baby in her arms, then shift their eyes through her when she catches them staring. Even the trucker, when he left Claire at the sliding glass doors, seemed suspicious of her capabilities. "You *sure* you don't need help?" he asked, and it was a point of pride to say no, a choice she refuses to regret now, though the halls are endless and the baby's weight (when did she become this strange, heavy person?) makes Claire's biceps tremble. She thinks of the high chair's heft in her kitchen, the muscular shake of putting it down and holding the baby and watching the crows dive toward their shadows on the grass. A natural instinct, she thought then. Something primitive guiding them to their own dark outlines, a shape that must have looked, from up above, like another self.

(*Push, Claire.* Sudden memory of a knife in her back, a knife pushing straight into her spine from the inside. Pain so articulate it felt poetic. *Back labor,* said the maternity doctor. *The baby's head is pressing on your spinal column. As she descends and turns, it will resolve itself.* But what if resolution meant Claire were split in half by the end? Already, she could feel the separation, one part of her in the grunting world of beasts, the other ghosting airily beside the bed. Her husband's hands pressed hard against her face, her salt-raw cheeks. *Push, Claire.* As if by sheer force he could hold her together.)

Claire blinks the thought away and steps onto an elevator. Her sleeplessness throbs, memories jangling incoherently. The walls inside the elevator are silver and sterile, and when the doors slide shut, she feels an odd comfort: everything contained. There is a teenage girl beside her, the type of girl so plain and familiar, she looks like déjà vu too. Auburn hair, as long as Claire's but untied and wild, frizzing broadly in the Texas heat, and irises the color of mud. (Raw umber: the name of the color coming to Claire's mind unbidden, the image

of a rolled-up tube of acrylic.) The girl looks exhausted. She stares at
the baby with red-rimmed eyes.

"What floor?" she asks Claire.

Claire isn't sure. "The speech clinic?" she guesses.

The girl pushes 10 without comment. As the numbers tick upward, she watches the baby snuggled against Claire's chest with a
strange look on her face. Desire or revulsion. A naked, intimate look.
The girl doesn't necessarily look like Evie. But she reminds Claire
of Evie. Something about the eyes, that horror-struck hunger—how
Evie looked when she looked at her bald mother, sleeping. Claire feels
the elevator lurch, a sudden tippiness, as if time has unhitched itself
from the world and is sliding them together along a rope much too
thin for the weight it carries. The girl seems about to cry. She stares
at the baby nestled sweet and tight against Claire's chest, and Claire
feels the urge to reach out, to comfort her. To mother. She reaches.

"What the fuck?" the girl yells, jumping away from Claire's hand.
"What are you doing?"

Claire winces back. "I'm just— I'm sorry, I didn't mean—"

"What are you, a fucking pedophile?" The girl moves farther
away from her, eyes skittish. She no longer resembles Evie, a girl (this
forgotten part suddenly returns) who was twice put on probation
at Briarfield for dishonesty. "Stay the fuck away from me," not-Evie
hisses, pressed hard against the silver wall, and the baby leans closer
to Claire's ear.

"*Arrêtes,*" she whispers. "*Laisses-la tomber.*"

It's only once the girl leaves the elevator that Claire looks down
and realizes her breast is exposed. It's just hanging there, outside the
border of her shirt: naked, foreign, a bald white globe with its blood-
dark pole, her pink blouse still unbuttoned from the baby's nursing
session in the restroom. Claire remembers the redhead's flinching dis-
gust. Imagines how she must have appeared to the girl, all these seams

of her body coming undone without her noticing. And yet the feeling that floods her as the elevator continues its rise is not the shame she expects—the humiliation of exposure, the sense that even this, a basic shirt, is too much for her to hold together. Instead, she feels oddly elated. She can sense something about to slip, but it's less herself and more like a costume falling off, a sticky pink husk sloughing at last. She feels a dark laugh rumbling deep in her belly, the kind of laugh the baby has sometimes. Nonsensical delight at the same thing happening over and over—a peekaboo game, a hiccup—a thing that gets funnier each time it returns until the baby is helpless with joy, with wet-eyed, gut-splitting caws of laughter at the same thing happening again, again.

ROOM 1001 IS EMPTY WHEN SHE ARRIVES. There is only a single bed, slightly rumpled, pale green covers thrown hastily over the pillow. Beside it, on the bedside table, a half glass of water, a pair of glasses, and a paperback book, spine unbroken: *The 7 Habits of Highly Effective People*. (Is she disappointed? She has to admit, if she had her choice, it would be Baudelaire, Rimbaud, at minimum a novel—though who is she to fault Pascal for seeking self-improvement?)

Claire sits on the blanket and runs her fingers lightly over the wrinkles on the pillow. She touches the dent where his head would be. The baby crawls to the end of the bed and pokes at a machine whose buttons make satisfying beeps. She squeals with delight and messes with mechanical programming that is probably important, that Claire should probably protect and doesn't.

They wait there, together on the bed, for a long time. No one comes.

The glasses on the bedside table are tortoiseshell. They remind

Claire of her husband's, but square instead of round. After they were married, Claire discovered his glasses were real. The prescription was so weak that he barely needed one, though of course the years worsened his eyes until he did. By the time he left her, eleven days ago now, he always wore them, the glass thicker, the distortion noticeable from any distance. The thought of her husband having sex with Gladys in glasses that he needs makes her feel inexplicably tender. She picks up Pascal's frames and puts them on, and the room goes impressionist— fuzzy slurs when she turns her head, the edges of objects feathering. Even the baby, laughing at the end of the bed, looks bizarre through Pascal's eyes, her pupils bulbous and dark, the scaly cradle cap magnified to the point of monstrosity. Claire takes off the glasses so quickly it dizzies her. She closes her eyes, feels the center of her body return. And when she opens them again, Pascal Duval is standing in the doorway.

He is tall and thin. Features as sharp as something whittled. Glossy black hair combed stiff with gel. He is carrying a newspaper in one hand, a manila file folder in the other, and he watches as she scrambles to get up from the bed, his expression so mild—curious, half-smiling—that she can't help but feel he's been expecting her. That she is somehow late to a meeting of her own design.

"Bonjour, Pascal," she says, and the baby looks up, startled by her French.

"Bonjour," says Pascal. His accent is decidedly American. He stands there in the doorway and stares at Claire for a long, held-breath moment. "And you are?" His English too sounds American. Something seems off about this, the same way something seems off about the dark suit he's wearing, and Claire doesn't know what to say. The plan in her head always ended at this moment, which was simply the moment of finding him and opening her mouth and hearing what came out. Being surprised by it, even. The way Pascal

must feel all the time, listening to the wrong language emerge from his lips; the way the baby must feel, even if the baby never seems bothered by it.

How did it happen? she might ask him. *What is wrong with you?*

Or perhaps: *What is wrong with the baby?*

What is wrong with me?

But to ask these questions seems suddenly impossible. Even to answer his—*And you are?*—feels impossible. Maybe dangerous. The edges of Claire's vision are flickering with dark, sleepless spots. Impressionist again, even without the glasses, and pulsing to the rhythm of her heartbeat. The way the man is staring at her quickens the flicker, and she suddenly recognizes, with a lurch in her stomach, how little the curve of his mouth looks like the newspaper photo, no longer that wry, clever specificity. More generically threatening. The baby raises her arms, reaching urgently for Claire. She curls up tight when lifted and stares at the man with skeptical eyes.

"You're not Pascal," says Claire.

"No," says the man. "I'm not."

"Do you know Pascal?"

The man laughs. "Do any of us *really* know Pascal?" Then he stops laughing, so abruptly that Claire knows it was never really laughter. "Tell me who you are," he says finally. "And what you are doing here." He stares at her down his aquiline nose, and she has that déjà vu feeling again—the sense she's been here before, that this man has followed her from somewhere else. But the feeling is gone before she can bring it into focus.

"My name is . . . Helen," Claire says. "I'm his wife." The words startle her, arriving without thought or warning, as if steering themselves. She thinks of her husband in the doorframe: *I just need to see where this goes.* "Please. Can you tell me where he is?"

But the man only blinks. "*Pascal's* wife?"

"He may not have mentioned me. Because of, you know. The amnesia."

"Right," he says slowly. "Right. And this is . . . ?" He gestures to the baby.

"My daughter. And Pascal's, of course."

The baby starts to cry. She lays her head against Claire's neck and whispers, *"J'ai fini, maman. Je suis fini."*

"Shh," says Claire, rubbing the baby's back. "It's okay. We are almost done. We are almost there."

"Nous y sommes," says the baby, weeping.

"You'll notice the resemblance, of course," says Claire.

The man doesn't reply. He just starts walking slowly toward her. Something about his face is changing, little by little—the eye sockets darkening, the angles sharpening. Beneath his jacket, a brief flash of silver at the waistband, and she thinks of the snub-nosed Ruger in her bedside table, thousands of miles away. But of course that would be crazy. For him to have a gun.

"Perhaps we should sit down," the man says, and inside his mouth, his tongue looks black. Though of course that's crazy too—a shadow. A trick of the eye.

"They say babies look more like the father when they're born," says Claire. "An evolutionary trait, so the male knows not to leave. Not to abandon their offspring. Have you heard that?" She knows she is babbling. But she's pressed against the bed, caged by machines on both sides, nowhere left to go. Besides, she can't seem to still her mind on the dark outline it keeps circling, the shadowy reason all of this feels like a memory. The black spots in her periphery are pulsing harder, taking shape: a flock of black spots, a fleet. "The apple and the tree," she says. "That's the phrase."

"I need you to calm down."

"Le pomme de arbor. That's how they say it in French."

"We could sit right here. I could hold the baby for you, and we could talk, nice and calm."

"Please," she says, and only when her voice meets her ears does she realize she's crying. "Just tell me where he is."

"You know I can't do that."

"Oh." She squeezes the baby tighter, but she's already squeezing the baby tighter, and the baby begins to yell. "Okay. Okay."

"Helen," says the man. "Give me the baby."

"It's okay, it's okay, it's okay."

And then it's not okay. Then the man is reaching for her arms, yelling for security. The feathers pushing out of his cheeks are glossy and sharp and growing longer by the second, and his eyes are all pupil, hair fluttering now with a hidden wind. He's trying to tell her something, she knows this, he's saying it over and over. But all she understands are the hands on her arms, hands on the baby, and the fury is a primal roar inside her, a roar without language— flash of fur, a savage yowl. Their jostling knocks the bedside table, and the water glass shards itself to pieces on the floor. Its fangs gnash open a memory: "I am doing this for your own safety," the man is telling her. "I am doing this for the safety of the baby." But with her arms pinned down, her body pressed hard against the bed, the safety hurts—and that dark outline looms, the thing she won't let her mind land on, that she can forestall as long as she holds her breath—

And then she's running. Aimless down the long hallways, a maze of fluorescent hospital corridors, baby tight in her arms, skin to skin. She doesn't look back but knows they're still there, the hands reaching for her, waiting to seize. She remembers just how it felt when they closed in on her: safe and then not, gentle and then not, until she could hold her breath no longer, until the darkness swooped, the sweet and silent release.

"THE APPLE DOESN'T FALL FAR," her husband said, looking down at the blankets in his arms. "She looks just like you, Claire. She's beautiful. She's the most beautiful girl in the world."

Claire was still rising up from the anesthesia. Her body was a cloud, blood a numb fog without borders. She hovered somewhere between the hospital mattress and the stiff white sheets. Later she would feel that same bone-deep knife stabbing her shoulder over and over, and the nurses would tell her this was merely the referred pain of gas, which they had pumped into her body during the c-section. It would astound her that trapped air could feel so much like dying. But right now, in the quiet enclosure of their private room, she felt nothing. She looked at the baby her husband was holding, and it looked like all babies, anonymous and pink. Impossible to know if it had come from inside her or if it was just any old baby, picked up from the nursery as he walked by.

This was the part where she was supposed to feel love. She knew that. She was supposed to hold the baby like the books said, skin to skin right after labor, and everything would click into place, that primitive connection. But what she felt was terrifyingly unintelligible. It was the feeling of reading and reading and suddenly realizing her eyes were just skimming over the words. It was the feeling of an empty canvas that everyone called hers when she knew the truth.

She said, "That's what you used to call me." Her words were hoarse, the first words she had spoken from this cloudy new body. Her previous words had been to ask the doctors for more time to push. Please, she had said as the beeping machines drowned out her words. Please, stop, I can do this by myself. But they had said no, and then they'd strapped her down, and then they'd put her under.

Her husband looked at Claire, lying in the bed, as if he were only now realizing she was there. "What did you say?"

"You used to say that to me."

"I don't remember."

"Helen. The most beautiful girl in the world. You used to call me that."

"Well, you still are. There are two of you now."

Claire closed her eyes and waited for the things she knew were coming. Mythic, magical things, all the things she had read about. The golden milk that would snake invisibly into her breasts. The tingling that would come back to her toes and sparkle slowly upward, like a million invisible fingers fluttering beneath her skin. The love that would gather a little bit at a time in her brain, at first just a collection of dissociated impressions—the scent of the baby's scalp, the iron-tight grip of her tiny hand—and then a sudden wholeness that would flood her with understanding. *A mother tongue,* they called it. Didn't they? Not something learned, not something she might be missing. It was inside her already, this love. Innate, pulsing firmly in the places she couldn't yet feel but would. For all she knew, it might be pressing itself right now against all her numb walls, running down her corridors and tunnels, the tangled networks of her body, thumping against each locked door, finding its own impossible way out.

"AND WHAT HAPPENED NEXT?" the little girl will say. "Did we get away?" Though of course she already knows. She will tilt her dark, tousled head on the pillow, curl her feet into eager parentheses and grab them with her hands, rocking back and forth. This is a bedtime story she loves. Romantic epic of birds and mystery, of secret corridors and flight, and the Crow Man with his wide wings—her favorite part—chasing them breathlessly down the halls. She knows the ending, but happy endings never fail to please, even when you know they're coming.

Claire will turn out the lamp and tuck up the covers. She will touch her daughter's hair, her chipped pink smile, and continue to find stray pieces of her phantom husband, the husband who will return and leave and return and leave for years to come, never able to decide A or B. Here, though, are his eyes: a burnt brown, shrewd and skeptical, and darker with every passing year. Here are his hands, delicate, golden in the night-light's cast, reaching for her. Here is his faith in the power of a story told with conviction.

"Of course we got away," Claire will tell her, smoothing her hair, her princess nightgown of palaces and horses. "I saved you, all by myself. Don't you remember?"

"But tell me. Tell the Crow Man part again."

"The Crow Man wanted to take you. He reached out with his shiny black wings. He opened his dark, dark mouth. And we ran and we ran, down every long hallway. I said to you, should we go this way? Should we go that way? Will we ever make it out? And you said, *Oui, maman! Oui!*"

"We!" The girl will laugh. "Tell me!"

"And we gathered speed. We were airplanes stuck inside, we were birds in a cage, we were ready for takeoff—"

"Tell me! Tell me who we were!"

"We were smoke, so fast they couldn't see us. We were superheroes, so fast they couldn't catch us. And we flew around and around those hallways, faster and faster—"

"Yes!" the girl will cry. "We! We!"

"Until we turned the corner and there they were, the doors to the outside, to the sky—and then finally—"

"Lift-off!" The girl will leap on the bed. She will come back down and wrap herself close, believing it will always be this way, that it has always been this way. "We, we, we!"

"That's right, my love. You and me. All the way home."

WHAT REALLY HAPPENS is they end up in a bar on Underwood Street, ten blocks from the hospital. Claire has lost the dark-suited man somewhere around a corner. She's lost her purse too, a realization that fills her with electric dread, her body a bright charge waiting to trip. The bartender takes one look and hands her a glass of water.

"Whiskey too," she says.

He glances at the baby. "Really?"

"Any kind. Straight."

A man sitting at the end of the bar, a thick-muscled trucker type with a wild mane of chestnut hair, looks up from his beer and stares. Then looks away, flushing, when Claire stares back.

The baby seems unfazed.

She sits on a pleather-covered stool, baby on her lap. The bartender brings the whiskey. Claire waits for the sound of a door opening, for someone to come in after her, but no one does. A wall-mounted television behind the bar scrolls local news; the world, impossibly, is continuing as normal. On the screen, a plain woman with dyed-red hair and flat cheekbones is talking cheerfully about a voter registration controversy. A two-alarm fire on Lincoln Street. A fungus in the lake water that continues to cause concern. Even on low volume, the news anchor's voice is garishly chirpy, but her eyes are as flat and empty as her face. She reminds Claire of the girl on the elevator, the girl who reminded her of Evie, all these girls pearled together into one long string of reminding, reminding.

The men at the bar aren't looking at the news anchor. No one else is paying attention when Pascal's face suddenly appears on the screen. It's the newspaper photo again. From this distance, his face is a smooth, flat gray, though Claire knows if she moved closer to the screen, it would dissolve into dots again, into pixels of dots. She asks the bartender to turn up the volume. By the time she can hear better, the photo on the screen is not Pascal anymore. It's a detective behind a microphone: pointy nose, chiseled features, glossy black hair Claire remembers for its texture as it brushed against her cheek by the hospital bed. Same manila folder in his hands; same crisp dark suit and Ruger at his waist. The Houston police, the anchor's voice explains brightly, are looking for Pascal Duval, who is not Pascal Duval but an American felon wanted for conspiracy and murder. His attempt at a new life—this amnesia business, this fictional blank slate—was nothing more than an old-fashioned scam. He is sought for questioning after leaving the hospital on foot last night, just as his story began to fall apart. He has not been seen since.

Channel Seven News will not be releasing his real name, as investigations are pending.

The words wash through Claire, and she knows she should understand more of them. But her ears catch only the shapes of the sounds, not the meaning. She waits for the flat-eyed news anchor to go on. To describe, with a condemning look into the camera, an unstable woman also wanted for questioning. A dangerous woman, a woman with a baby, a flight risk, a risk to others. A person of interest.

But the anchor's flat eyes look right through her, and her face is nothing but pixels dissolving into a smile that could be anyone's smile, and why don't we head over to weather with Gary—Hello, Gary!—and suddenly the story is finished.

(*No, the story can't be finished,* the little girl will pout. *Please tell me more.*)

The weatherman explains that a storm may be coming but also may not be coming.

(*Tell me who we were.*)

The lake fungus will continue to be a point of concern, related to runoff from the rains. Either that or pesticides; have we brought this on ourselves? The waters will continue to be tested.

(*Tell me who you are,* said the crow. *And what you are doing here.*)

As if it were ever so simple.

AND YET WHAT IS TRANSLATION without the attempt? Bend it this way, it's a tragedy. Bend it that way, it's a love story. So here it is, my love: the story of who I am. I'll put it down in a language you believe, I'll tell you the story as long as it takes, I'll tell it again and again, I'll tell it until you sleep.

Imagine, once upon a time, a woman. On a stool in a bar in Texas, holding her baby close. Imagine the ache: her biceps and back, the breasts heavy and hard with milk, the two-days-damp bra and the rancid blouse, feral and pink. The greasy forehead, greasy hair. The itch of unbrushed teeth. Imagine how it feels to be inside that body. To have no car, no answers, no way to move forward, no easy road back, just the cash in her pocket—not enough—and the exhaustion of mapping a safe route home.

Dark, winging thoughts. Headed darker, and nothing to stop them.

Until the baby looks up. She sees the panic on the woman's face. She reaches out her splayed, sticky fingers, presses her hands against the woman's closed eyes, her oily cheeks. "Mama," she says. "My mama." Imagine the chubby arms outstretched, wrapping tight around her mother's neck like the rope they've always been, a rope any mother would choose—the woman realizes this suddenly, with a certainty that stills her—again and again.

What would you have her do?

Perhaps she walks to the pay phone in the back of the bar. She lets the baby press the buttons (the simple joy of those beeps!) and holds her breath (a small hope, but at least in this moment there is still hope). She listens to the thump of the ringing line, a heartbeat looping its steady rhythm through hundreds of miles of wires across America, miles and miles to a ringing phone in an empty house. House of doors locked tight as mouths. House of crows on the roof and crows on the lawn. House of shiny windows the crows won't stop flinging themselves into all summer until somehow, finally, one day for no reason, they will.

The pulse of the line cuts to silence.

"Hello?" says a voice. "Is someone there?"

And maybe for a moment I'll let you believe what the woman in the bar wants to believe: that her husband has returned. That he is holding one end of that phone cord and waiting for her, a phantom on the other side of the country, to come home.

"Are you there?"

Maybe I won't tell you this: that when the line cuts out, it's not a man picking up but the phone company ending the call. That the hoarse, smoky voice she hears in the receiver is just her own voice, exhausted and unfamiliar, echoing. *Are you there? Are you there?* Maybe I'll let you listen for it with her, the happy ending I know you want, the kind of happy ending she's waiting for too—the answer to her own question, the sound of the words flying out of her mouth, their bright and shocking arrival.

CERTAINLY, IT'S NOT THIS KIND OF HAPPY ENDING:

She walks home. Slowly, along the shoulder of the Texas highway, the baby on her hip and the sky a flat ocean blue. The pavement ripples with waves of watercolor heat, and she steps over roadkill that looks strangely foreign—armadillos, she thinks, but flattened to gray leather husks. They remind her of suitcases emptied of their belongings. Which doesn't sound beautiful. But it strikes her as beautiful, as something she could paint with a cool-toned palette once she gets back to Troy.

When the first man stops, or at least the first to accept her conditions—only while the baby is sleeping, and only as far as Texarkana—it's the chestnut-haired trucker from the bar. He drives an unmarked silver rig that could be filled with anything. His face is pink and bucktoothed, eyes evasive in a way that suggests a lifetime of loneliness. But he is kind. He offers her water, fashions a makeshift car seat out of blankets with the ease of someone who should have been a father, although he says no when she asks about family. He might be lying. She can't decide if the lie would make him more or less attractive. When she holds him close, finally—in the grass of an empty lot in Texarkana, skyline smoldering with dusk and the baby asleep behind the windshield's glare—she is not thinking of her husband. She is not thinking of Pascal and whatever road he's on, somewhere out there on the borderless horizon. She is not thinking of the husk of her car on a nearby highway, of the calls she will make, the auto shop, the repairs and reparations, the missing purse mailed by some sidewalk Samaritan, the blank canvases stacked in a quiet, empty nursery in Troy. She is thinking, as he brings his body inside hers, of how two states can exist in a single city. She can feel the serrated edges of the thing always at her back, that dark, winging doubt, coming to rest inside her stomach and curling inward, a shape as round and smooth as her love for the baby, every part of her gathering tight around the exact contours of this comforting certainty: She is doing what she needs to do for both of them to survive. She is doing what mothers do.

Sing Me a Song

O N THURSDAY I was ready to leave my husband. On Friday I wasn't. So on Saturday I drove alone to his family reunion, slipping out of the house before he woke. I stole his truck, this gunshot-blue thrust of a ride—I craved a howl then, a shaking wheel—and left him the keys to my compact, a Post-it note (*meet me @ beach*), and the last morning bun to get his attention. The bun was clotted with cinnamon swirling into itself, wombed with the dark knots of raisins we loved enough to fight over, and I knew Desi would appreciate the gesture. I also knew he would pretend not to see any of it. For all these reasons, I was hungry on the drive, windows down, daybreak whipping emptiness through the cab.

I took the freeways from Ithaca, the bumpy back roads once I hit the Poconos. I'd been staying late in the lab for months at this point, crunching data on oceans that wouldn't stop warming, rising, trickster data, apocalypse trends that broke every one of my models. What I wanted was the stalwart tilt of land, the twists and turns of the wild mountain edges. It was early summer, the world blown open with green. Cicadas were humming, but barely, their fleeting hearts nearly spent. They were the seventeen-year kind, these cicadas: for weeks they'd been breaching their underground graves, flashing their new wings all over our neighborhood like expensive purses. I could feel them staring me down—all billion of them—from above, below, all around, always those blood-red eyes, always their whispers. I hated them. And I was completely enchanted with them. This was confusing but also familiar, that summer being caught in its own weird tide of back-and-forth.

Here is what I loved about them.

I loved the husks they left behind in the grass, little empty ghost versions of themselves.

I loved the way they clung to the hulking, beefy trees like lovers, then stabbed merciless holes into the branches to lay their eggs.

I loved how they chased Desi down every time he used the lawn mower. It was a brand-new mower, top of the line, and stupidly loud—an expense we'd argued about, an argument he'd won with the low-blow point that I was barely home anyway, and couldn't I respect the care he had for our yard, for the landscape of our lives? But he hadn't anticipated the cicadas, those tireless suitors, drawn lustily to the roar of his engine. When they landed on him, he'd spring to frantic, violent life, a body gone rogue, and I loved how much I loved him in those moments. How close I felt to him.

I loved knowing that in a few weeks, when all the eggs stuffed inside the tree branches hatched, little kamikaze babies would inch out, crawl along the branches, and throw themselves over the side. They would look like grains of rice in the air, like weddings before it all goes south. They would land in the grass and bury themselves in graves to be born, and for years we'd walk over them without even thinking of them. That is how fast we would forget them.

As for what I hated, I couldn't quite figure that out. Part of it had to do with how they knew—instinctively, in the dumb and perfect way of animals—exactly what to do with their bodies after seventeen years. How that switch of life just flipped on effortlessly. Or maybe it was their song I hated. Siren stuck in my head, trite alarm that wouldn't snooze. Maybe I resented them in the same way I resented Desi every morning at the buzz of his clock, which he always set to go off earlier than necessary, and which he always slept through until I punched him in the side.

Of course, this was also the summer the doctors kept telling us we were running out of time. So that was part of it too.

THE REUNION WAS at my mother-in-law's beach house on Cape May. A five-hour drive from Ithaca, and by the time I got there, most of the cicadas were behind me in the suburbs. At least it felt that way, just a few coastal stragglers here and there, hoary sailors who'd lost their moorings. I parked the car on the shoulder closest to the beach and stood outside for a while, listening. Though I'd left before dawn, I could tell that everyone inside was awake—all fifteen of my husband's cousins, all the little golden broods they had brought with them, the bright and early risers, the whole sweet, fecund, Catholic family tree flush with life. Only our branch blighted.

I wasn't ready to face them yet, so I walked to the water. Even at a distance I could hear them all laughing together within the house, the children loudest among them. Voices practically glinting in the light. Desi's youngest cousin, I knew, was pregnant with her fifth. Still nursing the fourth. *What was she thinking?* I'd heard my mother-in-law say on the phone, laughing, and I knew she'd say it again at the party, would probably say it directly to the thoughtless cousin. It was as careless and crushing and laughable a question as every question anyone had ever asked me about my own hypothetical children, back when they asked.

Now they looked right through me as if I were made of glass. Now they didn't ask, a silence so fragile I almost missed the questions.

So what are you waiting for? Tenure?

Must've been hard for Desi to leave the firm. But Portland's got nothing on Ithaca—what a place to raise a family, right?

Think he'll take the New York bar? Or does he still want to stay at home with the kids?

How long have you guys been trying again?

On the beach, the tide was coming in. I made sandal prints in the wet part of the sand, then backed away as the water filled them like little pots. I made some more. That endless advancement. The sun was burning my shoulders, and I could taste salt in the back of my mouth, and I knew I should go inside, but I was stuck on the way the ocean kept sweeping in to fill my footprints. How it seemed like each impression would be enough to hold an ocean, and yet inevitably the ocean that filled them would also wash them away, these outlines of myself that I couldn't stop making.

Here is what they don't tell you about fertility drugs.

They make you pimply so you hate the outside of your skin.

They make you hot so you hate the inside of it too.

They make you bloated and swollen with belly-centered weight gain that teases, that is always fluid, only fluid.

They make you nauseated and prone to diarrhea and PMS weepy, and all this when you are supposed to be having as much blazing-hot sex as possible.

This is my long way of saying I didn't bring a swimsuit to the reunion because I wasn't ready to show anyone my body. Only now I was regretting it. My shirt was linen and sleeveless, but it was very dark blue, and already the sun had plastered its cling in the places my skin was most tender: my underarms, the small of my back. I felt unsloughed and thirsty. On the beach, a few dried-out husks from the recent molting skittered. Some fresher bodies too, I saw, red eyes still glowing, wings flickering with every briny gust of wind. I picked one up, one not as squished as the others, and held it out in my hand until the breeze blew it off. It was lighter than it looked. I picked up another, and that's when I heard a voice behind me.

"If you pull off their legs," it said, "the head comes off too."

I glanced over my shoulder. At first I didn't see anyone, which spooked me. Then I looked down and saw a little boy at my back, contained in the outline of my shadow. He stepped beyond its border into sunlight. One of the kids of one of the cousins, I supposed, though I didn't know his name. Maybe six or seven years old—that age when it's hard to tell, though isn't it always hard to tell?—with a mess of honey-yellow curls and a Spider-Man rash guard already speckled with sand.

"Try it," he said. "Pull the front legs. The head pops right off. It will *blow your mind*. Get it?" He laughed.

I looked down at the cicada corpse in my hand and pulled on the front leg, because why not? The leg came off. The head stayed on. I looked back at the boy, who was frowning.

"I think it only works when they're alive," he said.

"You pull the legs off the live ones?"

"Maybe." He shrugged and hopped back and forth on his bare feet. "Okay, sometimes I do," he admitted breathlessly. "Don't tell my mom, though."

I thought of Desi then, couldn't help it: how he sometimes chomped the lawn mower right on top of the cicadas as he wove his slow, ceaseless paths back and forth in the grass. "They're asking for it," he'd tell me. "That's for killing the trees, you bastards!" he'd yell before smashing the mower down righteously. But I could hear pleasure too, with each grind of the motor's jaw around a carapace. That sweet, dark crunch.

"Maybe I *will* tell your mom," I said, and the little boy stopped hopping, startled. "That's cruel. You shouldn't be cruel."

He narrowed his eyes, and all of a sudden I could see some shadow of adulthood inside him, or the teenager he might become: mocking, pitiless, drawn to the casual brutalities I remembered from my boarding school days. (Those behind-the-back snickers; the snide comments calibrated to be secretive yet overheard. That girl, Lilith, we forced to the bottom of the pond. I remembered them all.) The boy and I stared at each other for a second, two seconds. We understood each other's hidden possibilities. Then he blinked and it was gone.

"It's hot," he said suddenly. "It's *so* hot." The way he said it made clear the heat was somehow my fault. "My feet are *burning*."

"Then you should put on shoes. See how I'm wearing shoes? I feel fine."

"That's because you're a grown-up, Aunt Nell."

I was taken aback that he should know my name when I didn't know his. But they all looked the same, those children of cousins: vaguely like Desi in a way that was familial, vaguely not like him in a way that meant none were ours.

"You should wear shoes on this beach anyway," I said, putting on my best grown-up voice. "You don't want to cut your feet. There's glass all over."

The boy laughed. "Of course there is!" he shouted. "Don'tcha know that sand is *made* from glass? There's glass all around us! We're surrounded by glass!"

He spread his arms wide like wings, spinning in circles.

"Don'tcha *know* that?" he said.

The waves came closer, snatching at our feet. The beach was still empty except for the two of us. Impossible on a Saturday so euphoric with sun, the sweet spot of morning, the sweet spot of summer, and yet it was true: there was no one else. We could have been the only people in the world.

"Sand's not made from glass," I told the boy, who was still spinning. "It's the other way around. Glass is made from sand."

"Not true."

"It is true. I'm a geochemist. I study how the ocean works, and the land too, and glass is made from sand."

"Oh, you think you know so much." After a while he stopped, dizzy and panting, and stumbled before falling happily backward. He moved his arms and legs like a snow angel, eyes squinted closed against the sun. "Bury me, Nell!" he said, and I felt my heart lurch heavily toward a memory, suddenly dizzy myself. "Bury me all the way up. I'll tell them all you buried me in glass!"

What else to do? Of course I buried him.

HERE IS THE MEMORY.

The day we came home from our last appointment. After the doctors walked us through all the charts—graphs and numbers and histories of my blood and hormones and urine, all the wine-dark tides of my fathomless body—after the specialist drew a picture of my uterus that looked suspiciously like an hourglass and pointed at things and said to us, *The sands of time simply move through women at different paces; have you considered other options?*—after they handed us pamphlets about surrogates and "Adoption After 40," Desi lay facedown in our bed and asked me to get on top of him.

"I'm sorry," I told him, "but I'm not exactly in the mood. Weren't you listening?"

"I don't mean fuck me," he said. "I mean get on top of me. Lie down on me." His voice was thick, muffled by the pillow.

I climbed on top of him. I covered his back with my stomach. I covered his arms with my arms.

"More weight," he said.

So I pulled up the duvet. When that wasn't enough, I pulled up the extra comforter. When that wasn't enough, I got out of bed and gathered all the blankets in the house—every spare set of sheets and his mother's antique quilts and the picnic blanket we used to take to the park and the pale blue baby blanket someone had crocheted at some point I couldn't bring myself to remember—and I spread them all on top of our bodies, a fleecy sea, a monstrous pressure. We lay there beneath it, immovable, until the sun dipped low, until the shadows of the trees inched up the bedposts and stretched their branches to dusk across the ceiling. In a week the cicadas would begin to nose their way into the light.

"More," he told me, and he was crying now, and my cheek was pressed into his cheek, and the rumble of his voice resonated all the way to my stomach as if the voice were mine. "Crush me, Nellie. It's not enough." And it wasn't.

"IMAGINE," SAID THE LITTLE BOY, "that you pointed your magic wand at an hourglass and said, *Make that sand disappear.*"

The boy was just a head now. The rest of his body was hidden beneath a smooth, round belly of sand that I had packed over him. Deep in this dark pocket we'd made, his tiny fingernails would be caked with dirt. His scabby knees would be powerless. The sun blinked noon-high, flushing his cheeks and forehead pink, and I could see now that he had freckles, and they were so fragile looking I wanted to kiss them, so tender I wanted to scream. But I didn't.

"Do you know what would happen?" he said.

"Yes," I told him. "The hourglass would be empty. You'd have all the time in the world. Or none of it."

"No," he said. "You'd lose the insides and outsides both. Because the walls are made of *glass*, remember? You'd make the sand go, but the walls would go too. Get it? I don't think you packed my feet hard enough, by the way."

Obediently, I pounded down the little cracks he was making in the sand above his toes. I flicked away the bits of husk and wing that were mixed in. Whenever I found a whole cicada body, which was happening less and less, I threw it as far as I could into the ocean. The ocean kept creeping toward us.

"They won't come back for seventeen years," the boy announced, looking hard at me.

"That's right," I said. "You'll be in college by then."

He nodded. Barely, because his neck was mostly covered now.

"Out of college, maybe." I smoothed the sand over his arms, his Spider-Man chest. "By the time they come back, you'll be a grown-up."

"I know." Something in his voice made me pause and look at him. This round, freckled face that looked like everyone I knew and no one I knew. "I've thought about that," he said quietly. "I'll be so old next time. I'll be a different person."

He closed his eyes. His mouth—was it just the light, a flickering shadow?—seemed to quiver with an emotion he was trying to hold in. I pulled my hands away, tried to picture what he must be feeling. But all I could sense was the physical. How good it must feel beneath that cool, wet sand. The crushing weight of the dark, like being in a womb: immobile, choiceless. Nothing you can do but release yourself to the bearings of nature.

"Why does that bother you?" I asked, though it felt like an unfair question. Of course no one wants to be a different person. Of course everyone does. He didn't say anything. We stayed like that for a while listening to the ocean coming closer, and the sound was soothing and varied, rising and falling like a lullaby—so unlike the constant alarm-clock drone of these last few weeks. So beautifully unsettled.

Then he opened his eyes and looked up at the sun, squinting. "It doesn't bother me," he said finally. "It's just that my head itches. Will you scratch it, Aunt Nell?"

I put my hands into his hair. The curls were pale and delicate, whorls as particular—as impossibly intricate and personal—as fingerprints. I felt the sand caught in the curls, felt it all sifting slowly through my fingers. "Is that better?"

"Yes, that's better."

"I'm not your aunt, actually. I think I'm your cousin-in-law. Once removed."

The boy laughed. "No. You're right here."

"That's not what *once removed* means."

"I know what it means. But you're too old for a cousin. I know who you are."

I would have kept arguing. Only I was tired of arguing and I was distracted by something on the horizon, near the house—a figure getting out of a car that looked like mine. "Want to see something cool?" the boy was saying, shaking his head back and forth in the sand. "Watch this!" But I was watching something else. The distant figure, vague against the brilliant blue surge of sky, was just an outline. And yet the shape was so familiar. It was the shape of my husband. I felt a flooding hope. I could already imagine it, the way his body would press against my stomach, a shadow matched with the thing that cast it. "Are you watching?" the boy said. He was shaking his head faster, drilling vigorously down, burrowing the last visible part of him deep into the sand. It was becoming harder to see him. I could feel in my throat the need to call out to the far distance: *Where have you been? I have been waiting for so long.* "I'm doing it, Nell!" the boy cried, "I'm doing it myself!" And after a while I realized it was true: the sand had covered his ears already, his freckled cheeks, he was going deeper. Any moment now—still this faraway shadow walking toward me, coming into view—the sand would reach his closed eyes, the corners of his mouth. It would fill up all the empty spaces, like the ocean filling up each footprint. In a minute, the rest of him would be gone. In an hour, the tide would wash this spot entirely away. For years to come, we might walk over it and never know, our feet blissfully cool in the frothing water, what we were passing over. In some unknown quantity of time, I could rise and walk toward it, this body coming closer, waiting to be recognized.

Ten Kinds of Salt

The summer the animals began to disappear was the summer of the pink fires. Everything a little more alive than usual because that's the way of things just before they end—the muscular blaze of deer, for instance, in the headlight glare of highway cars. Crack of beers thumbed open at the edge of the shed that would later burn to ash. Foamy secrets we drank so fast our moms would never see, and the scald in our eyes, forcing it down, the belief that something better would arrive before the ache, and no fire like that could last for long.

Is this the world of all girls? Maybe. But back then, we had invented it.

Back then, our world was Hannah and Lana, Lana and Hannah, best friends forever and the necklace to prove it. Our world was sleepovers where we didn't sleep and baby doll dresses that made us the opposite of babies and dolls. Our world was trading vintage Heartthrob cards until their black-and-white faces bent from handling: This is the boy you will marry. This is the boy who will leave you. (*Be gentle with them,* warned Hannah's mom, from whose closet we'd stolen the Heartthrobs. *They're fragile. They're still very special to me.* By which Grace meant the cards, though we liked to pretend she meant the boys, how sad, how pathetic in such a mom way, and laugh.) Anyway, we always made sure we ended up with our soul mates—Hannah's vampy Trevor, my bad-boy Jake—and then it was Miss America pageants on repeat until my dad kicked us out of the den. Our world, back then, was watching: a constant vigil for color, for buzz, for the bright sequins of our real lives, stuck on pause until we could at least get cell phones. Which is maybe why that summer, the summer I turned thirteen, the summer Hannah came home from boarding school, our world was also Peter McCleve and all his dead animals brought back to life.

Peter's shed was full of them: foxes with Farrah Fawcett bangs, beady mascara-blacked raccoons. Owls and turtles, silvery fish painted shiny as lip gloss, everything gutted and salted and sewn back up into newly unbroken bodies. The squirrels alone formed a mounted, buck-toothed army on the plywood shelves—squirrels in mariachi outfits, squirrels in orange hunting vests clutching tiny rifles, squirrels yanking open their own furry chests to reveal superhero logos underneath. Peter was a specialist (he told us) in reincarnating the dead. And if you're going to return, why not come back as something better than you were, something that also makes a buck at the Sacramento craft fair? Hence the groundhogs retroed out as Jem and the Holograms, sticker-star earrings pressed into the fur, and Pizzazz, my favorite, in a neon green cotton-ball wig at the front. Hence the mounted bass with human teeth—dentures Peter's grandma was going to throw out—leering at us with a witchy, white grin.

And then there was Peter himself, the most miraculous rebirth.

He was twenty-one now (locked up for five years), and the pale, pimply kid we remembered from bus stops had become a man, golden with thick-armed smolder. We knew the rumors. A drunken joyride, alone, at sixteen. Hit-and-run, cops tracing the crushed car back to his driveway; then juvie, rehab. Now he lived with his parents and fancied up animals in the backyard shed, and maybe there were jobs that would have impressed us more. But there was something mythic in him, in his own resurrection. Something that made us want to push the T-shirt up his hard, knobby stomach and look for the sewn-tight scar.

"You'd be surprised," he told us, leaning his threadbare jeans against the workbench. "You'd be shocked, actually, at how much people will pay for roadkill if you just give it a shine."

"It's an awful lot of roadkill," Hannah said, rubbing her arms. She made it seem like she was cold, but I figured she liked him watching her touch her own skin. I wished I'd thought of it first. "Is it really all from cars? You don't shoot some on purpose?" She nodded at the hunting rifles in the corner.

"What do you think?" he said.

What I thought—what kept me up late—was Peter running his hands across each shiny rifle. The shed's doorframe dug into my spine, but still I leaned harder. I was trying to summon tautness, that slim and nimble way of moving that Hannah had learned from her dancer mom, or maybe brought back from their fancy school in Boston, where Grace had gone too. There Hannah was considered a *legacy*, a word she always said in embarrassed italics but which made me think of delicate heirlooms passed lovingly between generations—austere family pearls, slender lockets, the haughty white profiles of cameo women. In the shed, I tilted my face. I put my hands behind my back, arched so Peter could see my flat stomach, the silver belly button ring winking out beneath my shirt, if he looked. He didn't

look. "I think you wouldn't shoot a little animal," I said, and liked
how it sounded.

"The little ones are hard to shoot."

"But you think about it, don't you?"

I could feel Hannah staring at me with a funny look, a who-the-
hell look. Same look I probably gave *her* when she stepped off the
plane with her actual breasts and satin hair the color of fawns, plus
those weird new loafers she wore despite the heat. *They all wear them
there,* she'd said, then let her eyes skitter out the airport windows to a
far-off place, a Boston place, a place that made her profile go all red-
brick and wistful. And me stuck forever in Plainsville, Mouse Brown
Frizz Town, Boobie Flats—dead suburban Sacramento where she'd
left me. Though it was hard to stay mad with her doctor dad still
away in Syria, plus her mom in one of those moods. Harder still when
Hannah put down her backpack and cried delicate tears into my hair
at Baggage. *I just missed you,* she said, holding me tight, and I felt forgiveness unclasp in my throat: fragile, returned to me, legacy, legacy.
Tell your mom thanks for picking me up.

"What I'm thinking about," said Peter, still not looking at my
belly ring, "is gutting this chipmunk." He picked up a razor and the
tail of something gone ratty and matted. "Feel like watching, girls?"

Perhaps this is worth noting: Peter's razors miracled ugly to
beautiful. He slaved over those corpses—rinsed entrails from the skins
before preserving them, worked relaxers into the fur, blow-dried on
low so the hair would fluff without burning. He brought crushed,
gray lives back from the dead in a way that felt spiritual. His post-jail
body was the finest example of this, all the pale tanned out, all sinew
and shine, muscular as the curve of a revved car. *Vehicular manslaughter,*
Hannah had whispered outside the shed. *I heard it was a girl.* Did it
thin out the syrupy feeling we felt around him? If anything, the edge
of salt made it sweeter. If anything, what we'd wanted our whole

lives was exactly this: Peter's fingers sunk in the downy dark of the chipmunk's belly, the blood and guts, the real mess of the thing—then emerging, finally, with one bright heart, round and impossible as a pearl.

"Want to hold it?" he said, and every hand inside of me opened at once.

Which is why we were willing, in the weeks that followed, to do the dirty work—me scraping the pavement for squirrel donations, Hannah holding open the plastic bag. Her voice cooing up each time into a gaspy spiral so thin and breathy ("ew ew ew EW EW"), it was almost pretty by itself, just one more reminder that we weren't the same anymore, not really, and we both knew it even if we never said it out loud. I felt lots of things about this, but one of them was grateful. So I carried the shovel.

Picture us, then. Hannah and Lana, Lana and Hannah, Target bags of fresh roadkill swinging beside our smooth thighs, our nicked-up knees, as we make our way toward romance. Picture a summer we knew even then we'd remember for its bloody costs, but also its returns—how it feels to be tank-top-bare and June-loosed, out of the houses where dads hit (mine) or dads leave (hers) and moms swirl from room to room lonely with wine, where no one cares what you do as long as you show up alive for dinner. Remember freedom. Remember the sweetgreen smell of scattered grass cuttings and the hair-whipping joy of biking without helmets, remember the roar in your ears, remember tonguing the sweat from the tiny cup above your lip. Remember disconnection—no Facebook, no Finsta, no translucent life on a screen, just life as it felt in your teeth, raw and thick and throbbing with everything you could ever want, so sun drenched and pretty, it could make you scream, want to tear through something just to hear it rip.

Picture us like that.

II

Twenty nights before the night of his death, Peter McCleve was watching the sky. It was that electric time between day and dusk, sun barely sunk, horizon a long orange power cord in front of him. Peter wanted to feel the jolt. He'd been like that once, a long time ago, the type to stop and take notice: blue starlight a chord in his chest, the tawny California hills so curled and animal-like, he used to see them breathing. Hard to remember a world like that, the sky something other than merely empty—though he was trying, searching beyond his windshield for a vision that hadn't yet appeared. He wasn't sure what it was, only that something had told him, *Get in the truck,* something had said, *Keep your eyes up.* So he did, and drove.

His heart beat a funny itch inside its bars of bone—Peter tried to shake the sensation. It had been coming on more often lately. That hot, frantic feeling of a cage inside him.

He knew himself well enough to know that maybe he wasn't searching the sky for anything. That maybe this ride on this night, his twentieth-to-last night, was more about getting away from the little shed off the back of his parents' house. He liked to call it his *studio,* and when the girls were there, when he looked around through their eyes, he could almost believe that's what it was. But at night, by himself, the room was too close and tight, smelled too much of death. Too much a shed.

He knew too that this aimless ride might be more about getting away from his parents' basement and the bottles they kept there, bottles that sang to him like bells, ringing their empty promises. Bottles they could have trashed for his sake but didn't. *You need to live in the world, Peter, and it's not spinning around you.* His mother had told him that once, watching him unpack his few things from rehab. *You need to live in the world, and the world has booze in it. So deal.*

So deal. He sighed, tightened his grip on the wheel, and drove in long loops through town. Night was leaning in, the road brightening by contrast in his headlights: dark begets light, light begets dark. A balance he didn't yet understand, though he was trying. He thought of the Eleventh Step prayer. *It is by self-forgetting that one finds. It is by forgiving that one is forgiven. It is by dying that one awakens,* and suddenly there it was, a flash of white in the periphery of his vision. He felt the truck start to swerve beneath his hands, felt the gallop spring into his chest like a fenceless deer—wings? A glimpse of gold amid downy white feathers, the blur of a lost thing returning?

He understood then, impossibly and unequivocally, that what he was seeing in the corner of his vision was the owl he'd mounted last week, the white snowy owl with golden eyes he'd tried to replicate with marbles and couldn't. It was the owl (he thought all of this so quickly, it was as if he had already known it) that had been missing from its place on the workbench for three days, the owl Grace hated because he'd dressed it as a bespectacled doctor. The owl whose eyes he couldn't get right, no matter how much he tried; whose eyes mattered because they reminded him, the honey color smudgy with death, of a memory that kept flapping away.

And then, just as quickly, the owl was nothing more than a wisp of cloud wafting by. The edge of a storm coming into view—they had said that on the radio, hadn't they, that a storm was coming, and Peter's thoughts thudded hard back into this world, the one that didn't spin around him. The wheel sweaty in his grip, the itching in his chest: he felt feverish. Felt the urge for Grace like a drink, that cool thin swallow of her body, and he understood suddenly where he was driving although she said never to come to her house, that she'd always meet him in his shed. He'd be quiet, he promised himself. He'd signal to her somehow from the driveway. She would wave him off and he would drive back home and she would walk to his shed

and offer the forgetting she offered him, sweet hard slugs of forgetting, and he knew this and drove forward with a clear purpose. Not
watching the sky for wings. Not watching her house for a face in
the upstairs window, a girl wondering who he was, this scattered,
shaking, blurry boy behind the wheel, wondering shouldn't someone
drive him home?

III

Because her bed, with its smooth, unwrinkled, un-moved-on sheets, felt
like a long letter Grace couldn't write. Because Xanax, Zoloft, Pexeva,
Zyprexa: old poem of darkness, those decades-long stanzas, and Peter
as blank as a new verse. Because not knowing when, or if, her husband
would return; and because she loved him, which should have meant no;
and because she could kill him a thousand ways with her mind, which
meant yes, yes, any means of survival. Yes.

Because sleeplessness.

Maybe because the way the skin beneath her eyes was changing.
Grace had never taken note of that skin before, never even considered it because it was just skin, the thing covering up her muscles,
her face, her open-eyed way of smiling—yes, her beauty, although
beauty wasn't quite the point. Once, skin had been merely a reliable
way to clarify her muscles' movement. What had happened? There
was something papery now beneath her eyes, crinkly and thin as
checkout-lane magazines. Her neck too—folds where there'd never
been folds before—and her veiny hands, old-woman hands, not the
hands of someone in her late but athletic forties. She'd been proud of
her hands once. Choreographer's hands. Taut, elegant, but secretly
strong enough to lift a dancer, to point to a troupe and transform
them into something synchronous and otherworldly, unencumbered
by mortality. When was the last time she'd felt that power? She had

made the mistake, Grace realized now, of believing she held a gravity deep within her, one the outside world would always orbit.

But nothing held. Everything slackened, threatened to scatter. Eyes, neck, traitorous skin. Traitorous brain, her focus as fluttery as loosed birds. On her desk, stacks of scratched-out pages for a company in San Francisco, a long-overdue ballet commission—the type of choreographic work on which she'd made her name. The type of work that shouldn't be hard. But the bodies she sketched were nothing more than fragments, mere vignettes. A useful sequence here and there, but none of it adding up to the whole she needed.

Even her husband was in pieces these days, Matthew's voice disembodied in a war zone across the world. Syria this time—an operating theater near a rebel base that was frequently shelled—although she sometimes worried she'd forget where he was, his philanthropic benders frequent enough to blur. On weekends he'd call from satellite phones that Doctors Without Borders provided for family check-ins and stateside clinical consults, each type of call pulling battery life from the other. And so Grace felt the pressure to rush, to tell him yes, of course her meds were up to date, and no, they weren't affecting her focus, the commission work was going great, and yes, Hannah was happy at school, of course she called home nightly, of course. Which might have oversimplified some facts. But there was that phone battery ticking down against some other person's life, someone who needed saving. Besides, how much of what she said got through to Matthew at all? His own stories were hopelessly incomplete, shattered by the patchy reception. *I'm telling you, Grace, if you could only see xxxxxxxxxxxxxxx. A boy last week who xxxxxxx and one leg. The xxxxxxxxxxxxxxxxxxxxx unmendable. My God. xxxxxxxxxxxx your perspective, you know? And the xxxxxxx to survive. We are so lucky, Grace, so xxxxxxxxxxxxxxxx. Remember that.*

And she did. The trouble, in fact, was that she couldn't forget.

xxxxxxx and one leg. xxxxxxx and one leg. Those crumpled piles of
paper on her desk. Bodies that stubbornly refused to fuse, to make
any sense at all. Late at night, across the empty stage of her bedroom
ceiling, the Operating Theater filled in Matthew's blanks, cast show
after show without her permission: sliding white spotlights of incoming
shells, the severed arms and rolling heads. The craters. Right at that
exact moment, perhaps—right now—no, right *now*—all her husband's
exhausting goodness could be arabesquing into tiny, unmendable
pieces as the bombs came down. She watched as her mind made it
happen again and again, horrifying but necessary. She knew it was
impossible that her mind would project the exact same thing that was
happening on the other side of the world—no magic here, after all—
and so as long as she remained vigilant, watching the terrible show,
she knew Matthew must be safe.

Because that kind of thought had begun to seem logical. Saving
him by destroying him.

On the worst nights, it wasn't enough to shatter Matthew, and
her mind drifted to Briarfield, to Hannah—not the sweet girl Grace
had sent there but the stoic young woman taking her place, the one
who looked more and more like her mother, and who called less and
less as the year went on. That tender softness of her newly adolescent
body: hard pear of her girlhood gone suddenly lush, easy to bruise.
Hannah had always been an obedient child, unassuming and too
eager for approval, the type to apologize before the affront. And what
Grace could picture in the gaps between calls was how mercilessly
Hannah must have been split open by the girls of Briarfield, girls
with blade-sharp judgment, girls who'd take down one of their own
before risking their loss in a crowd. Night after night on her bedroom
ceiling, Grace watched Hannah cry alone in her distant dorm room.
Watched her slip out the window after lights-out and take long walks
through the thorny woods, that pocked white moon scoffing down

from above. She always made her lonely way to the edge of campus: the forbidden pond and its dark allure, its tenuous reflections that gathered and split, gathered and split. Sometimes she wandered to the end of the dock, running her hands along the frayed seams of reeds at the edge, and looked down into the black water below. What would make a person do it, what would be enough of a reason? Grace's mind walked right up to the edge of that thought before she panicked, stepped back, her only relief the late-night phone call she swore she'd stop making, swore this was the last time. And Hannah's voice on the line, safe and sound in her dorm bed, was always the same: sleepy, a little impatient, mostly embarrassed. *Mom, seriously? You woke up my roommate again.*

So here was another reason then. Besides the papery eyes, the flinty crackles of satellite static; besides scratched-out ensembles and reuptake inhibitors and the *xxxxx* and the *xxxxx*. Because when it wasn't enough to imagine the worst, Peter filled the emptiness. Because when he held her hips, her thighs, held every loosening part of her in hands that were far from elegant—hands that were dirty and gut crusted, hands that looked like the shame she tried to summon and couldn't—Grace felt a force center deep inside her, a darkness so potent that light was no longer the point. She was gravity itself. She was a crater, already shelled; she was the drop beneath the Gorge Bridge; she was the black abyss of a long-ago pond. Not threatened, but the threat. Not waiting, not anticipating: she was already there. There. *There.* She'd guide Peter's hands, she'd bite his neck. *There, there, yes. Like that.* And when she came, it wasn't the falling apart of making love to her husband. More like focused reassembly: that black hole inside her, sucking the rest back in.

Mid-June now. The nights were shorter, the arrangements more careful. For a time, an invisible clock had been ticking toward school vacation—Hannah's impending return from Boston and Grace's certainty that this would mean the end of Peter. Grace would be busy reconnecting with her daughter. They would stay up late in the summer-lit nights, lie on her bed and wait for Matthew to call from Syria. They would talk about Briarfield, all the things Hannah seemed too busy to discuss on the phone: the teachers, the dorms, the girls and the boys. How some things had changed in these decades between them, and how some had stayed the same.

But more often than not, Hannah slept over at Lana's. (*That's okay with you, isn't it, Mom? I mean, she really missed me too.*) And so the clock ticked onward, the nights as empty as before. Days too stretched out blank and inessential: the girls carried their own house keys, made their own lunches, walked themselves to the grocery store. If Grace offered a ride, they were quick to establish their distance—no more begging to push the cart or scavenging her purse for quarters. No more please, please. Now they led with bared collarbones, jeweled flip-flops spanking their heels as Grace trailed behind them with an empty basket. They selected licorice ropes and lipstick, tipped their blown-straight heads in consultation over rainbow rows of Wet n Wild, and paid with their own dollars. Later, at home, they painted their toes on Hannah's comforter. They flipped through fashion magazines and rated the models while Grace watched through a crack in the door. Lana's merciless sneer—sharp white teeth, that glinty laugh as she slid her licked finger across the women's faces—always reminded Grace of Briarfield. And Hannah's pressed lips, her inscrutable smile, hair falling forward before Grace could interpret it: yes. That reminded her too.

The girls left polish streaks on the navy blanket. Hazy shimmers of Cherry Delish, of Flaming Orange Firestorm. After they were gone for the night, Grace would scrub at the stains with acetone, almost hoping they wouldn't come out. In another season (already she could see it coming), this might be a spot she would need to return to, a place to press her fingers against the shine—legacy of Hannah, glitter ghost on the smooth sheets. That aftermath sparkle, like the broken moon in water.

Grace stood up. Dusk had fallen at some point—behind the blinds she could see night stacked in thin layers—and she tried to squelch the urge to walk to the shed. She stood and looked at herself in Hannah's mirror, smoothed the wavy tangle of her black hair. (Not even one thread of silver, she reminded herself—there was that.) Dabbed from a pot of Hannah's gloss, ran it over her lips. (Pinkish without stain—there was that.) Then gloss beneath her eyebrows, a little more along the sharpest rim of her cheeks; she'd been stealing the fashion magazines the girls left behind, and she found beauty tips she'd never needed when she'd bought them herself but which proved surprisingly helpful now. This is how you make yourself look more awake: line the bottom rim of your eyes in white. This is how you make yourself look less old: don't smile when you apply the blush. This is how you make yourself look defined: put the shine along every bone. There. Like that.

IV

We burned things. Mostly to help Peter get rid of the entrails and the bodies too crushed to salvage, but also trash and old papers, knuckled branches, piles of leaves we could have jumped into but didn't. Stuff the world felt too full of already; we'd pile it all into tiny mountains and send their skylines flaming. From Peter's fire pit, the black smoke slow-danced itself toward blue, a loose-limbed sky, unbuckled with heat and waver, and if we could take all the trash in the world and make it *that,* then we were doing something good, weren't we? Burning off this ugly residue of being alive.

It's what I sometimes pictured now in the silence of my bedroom, the way I used to picture Peter and his guns. Those fires. I imagined myself getting closer to the flames and melting away my outsides, a golden toast that takes patience, like browning a marshmallow slowly instead of shoving it hard into the heat. The crust of me darkening and darkening and then falling away—everything pure underneath, that lightness I could feel at my core but no one could see.

"Watch this," Peter said once to Hannah and me. "I have something magic to show you." It was almost twilight, the fire burned almost to nothing; our moms would wonder about us soon, but how could we leave now, of course we could not leave. We watched him jog back to the shed, those little dots of fireflies in his wake, eerie green and disappearing as soon as you looked at them.

We didn't speak while we waited. I remembered how we used to be good with silence, back before Hannah left for school, before she came home and the silence felt different. Once, someone told me love means not needing to speak to someone because you're two halves of the same brain. It was an idea I remembered there by the fire, an idea that felt just right, like a heart necklace broken, lightning-ripped down the middle—Hannah and Lana, Lana and Hannah, twin halves matching up our jagged sides. I felt tears brinking, though if you'd asked me why, I couldn't have explained. I would have said it was the smoke.

Then Peter was back, jogging through the darkening field. He was carrying one of his white-powder jars, and he stood right next to me, breath heavy, his skin almost touching mine as he opened it. He said, "Don't try this at home, girls." And when he winked, it flared in me like the fire flared when he threw the powder on the coals and it all burst into hot-pink flames. I heard Hannah gasp, felt her breath go in as if it were my own. I felt the jar in Peter's thick hands—the cold of the metal getting warmer where he held it, the tiny bumps in the brass of the lid's ring, the way one part of the jar was made for another part and everything could screw right down to its proper place if we wanted to close it, to save it. I felt the pink fire because I had always felt it, because it was me. The whole night ballooning with oneness.

"What *is* that?" Hannah said, and her voice sounded hexed, and I felt that too.

Peter shrugged, but he looked pleased. "Just a weird kind of salt. I have a bunch in the shed, probably one for every color. It's really for the animals, to line the skins after I gut them. Salt dries the skin out so the bodies last forever. But it has this nice side effect on fire." He sprinkled more and the flames glittered: sunsets, sequins, the dress on Miss North Carolina, that horsey girl I'd pegged to win last week who came in second.

"My dad used to make bonfires," Hannah said after a while, and I glanced at her, wishing she'd shut up about parents. "When I was little," she added. "Not colorful fires like this. But bigger." She was staring at Peter with a weird look, unblinking. I didn't know what to make of it.

"That sounds nice," Peter said. He wasn't looking at Hannah, hadn't noticed what I'd noticed, but maybe he sensed it because his gaze went skyward, aimed pointedly away. His eyes were cast black in the shadow of his cheekbones. All around us, night began to pull its shade.

Finally, he said, "I used to do this with my band friends. A long time ago, before they stopped coming over." He cleared his throat. "Fires like this. We were your age, I guess. We burned up all kinds of things. I don't even remember them now. Copper pipes will turn it green, I think, or maybe blue. And that fake blood-pressure salt my dad always used at dinner—that made purple, I remember that for sure. I used to swipe it and watch him look around and yell at my mom for not getting it at the store. I never said anything."

"Why not?" Hannah said.

"What?"

"Why didn't you say something? When you saw what was happening?"

I poked her. She didn't poke me back. Peter sighed and I felt the held-together center finally scatter, tossed loose as salt. "I should have. It wasn't really that purple. Anyway, I thought you girls might like it."

I said, "You're really good with destruction," and he laughed. Then Hannah said, "What happened to your band friends?" and he stopped laughing, and I felt rage flare violently in my stomach. She had to know it was exactly the wrong question, part of the dead-eyed thing we saw in his face as we spied on him from afar. We had watched him do everything at this point, for weeks—eat cereal and sit in front of a dark TV and piss behind uncurtained windows. We had measured our days by the length of his summer shadow as it crossed the yard from the house to the shed. We had memorized his life. We had bought our way into it with flattened bodies, scraped intestines off the asphalt and felt shimmery flies throwing themselves against the taut white plastic of the bags we carried, we had smelled the smells, we had done it all to get here, to this new, perfect moment, pink flames, skin to skin, his dark voice filling us like smoke—and just like that, she had thrown on the lights.

"I guess people get older," he said. "I don't know. We grew apart. You two should get home, huh?" And he turned and walked away, back to his unlit shed. Night true dark by then, all the magic in the air hollowed out, and I wanted to do something spectacular and glittery, a thing that would summon him back to us, magical as pink fire. I wanted to shove Hannah forward into the coals and watch her blister. I felt these wants equally, the beautiful and the ugly. But I didn't do anything, and Hannah just kept staring at the fire, which was mostly gone now anyway.

"Hey," Peter said suddenly, looking back at us from the edge of the shed. "Have you girls seen my owl? The white one with the gold eyes?"

"You mean the doctor owl?" I said. Hope licked at my heart, flickering joy to have him turn back. "I love that one!"

"Yeah." He hesitated. "It's gone missing. The fox has too, I think—the one in the houndstooth coat."

I heard Hannah chuckle and turned, something snagging in my head before it made it to my mind. But she wouldn't look at me—still smiling, her eyes cast down at the coals, at her stupid shoes—and after a while I shook my head. "I don't think so," I said.

Peter waited there as if he wanted to say something else. But he didn't, and we didn't either, and then he faded off into the dark.

Later, on the walk home, dragging our feet now because we knew we were in trouble, I asked her, "Why was it funny? Those missing animals?" The snag I had felt suddenly kinked into a knot of realization, a terrible hope: "Did you take them?" Because it made as much sense as anything. The owl, in particular, looked weirdly like her dad, still abroad doing doctor-hero things, though my mom pegged him for a regular deadbeat. *Who leaves his wife for months?* she'd mutter. *Not to mention when she's in a state.* Which I guess meant the way Grace wore bathrobes these days, or watched us sometimes through the crack in the door while we played MASH and Heartthrob and seriously, Grace, don't think we can't see you there. Her crazy-lady hair so pathetic, we couldn't even laugh at her anymore. I could see why a husband would stay away. More to the point, I could see why Hannah would want the owl. I pictured her secretly running her fingers down those shiny white feathers in her room, holding her father and Peter to her chest at the same time, and I felt a new distance yawning between us, and not a small amount of awe. She always got what she wanted.

But she just shook her head. "Of course not. As if my mom would let me keep something that dirty. He probably just lost those animals."

The moon in the sky was a blank white face turned half away. "Nothing disappears without a reason," she said.

"So why did you laugh?"

"Are you kidding? A *fox* in a *hounds*tooth coat? A missing doctor?" She laughed again, and her eyes were in shadow the same way Peter's had been. "It's just funny sometimes. How death imitates life. Isn't that what they say?"

V

Why should he feel haunted? Why now, that pull of the past on his coat sleeve, just when he was starting to see a glimmer of future in Grace, a way of starting his life over? And yet *haunted* was the word that kept winging through his mind. The feeling of being watched—in the shed hunched over each tiny body, at home moving mindlessly from room to room. Even out in the woods, even when he *knew* he was alone, he couldn't shake those golden eyes staring at him from the trees.

And that empty space on the shelf. How every few days, a new space bloomed: the missing fox. Then the missing goldfinch. The top-hatted trout that swam off into nothingness, leaving its pine mount still tacked to the wall, and those three bandit squirrels in a single night—vanished, a pack of furry convicts on the lam.

What he felt first, oddly, was envy. It was still a fresh scar, his own barely healed ache for transformation. He could remember his cell door with its eight-inch window, the sound of the latch clicking and his heart like that hamster he'd had as a child, the one that went rabid and threw itself against the cage until it had a seizure and died. He could remember every part of him wanting to shrink down to a thing that could crawl out an eight-inch window, that could float right through a door. Hate of the body and its thick, inexhaustible solidity. Even after juvie, once he broke his probation and landed in rehab, there was still that sense of his body being too full, too stuck to the earth, without the lightness of liquor to unmoor him. He wanted air; he wanted to disappear.

Hence, irrationally and rationally, the envy as he looked at those empty shelves. It was so easy, apparently, to slip off into nothingness.

Mostly, though, he just felt haunted.

It got so bad he started asking the girls if they wanted to hunt with him in the woods. And he knew it was wrong, knew Grace would kill him if she ever found out. Of course he knew that kids shouldn't be around guns, even the air rifles quiet enough for suburbia. He tried to convince himself that it was a gift of education he was giving to them: the beauty of a sunrise, the liquid ripple of distant birdsong. But really, he was just afraid of being alone. Alone, there were too many things he remembered.

For instance: alone, he would come upon the Gorge Bridge at the edge of the woods, the bridge he had to cross every day to get back to his car, and suddenly the vision of Grace would be there looking down, transparent as a ghost. She'd be standing on the railing of the bridge, toes curled over the metal lip, the same spot he'd met her three months ago while hunting, that spot right above the deepest, emptiest space in the gorge. He hadn't understood at first that she meant to jump, and for a moment as he'd looked up at her, he had simply thought her magical. Immortal. Untethered by the earth, a windblown nymph floating in the middle of the cool spring woods. He would remember the yellow cotton dress clinging to her chest and stomach like a film, everything else ribboning out into the open air behind her, and the slim white arms, the bare white legs exposed as her skirt took the breeze, sun splintering across her face: all ethereal light. The only dark, earthly thing about her was her hair, black and glossless, a negative space he could fall into. (He had known even then, even in that first narrow moment of seeing her, that he wanted to bury his face in it, this hair that would later tangle in his mouth, choking him in a way that felt holy.)

Three months later it would have been a beautiful memory if his mind let him see it as it had actually happened. He could have remembered the way she turned to him and said *Please, go away* in a voice that seemed oddly polite given the circumstances. He could have remembered how he put down his gun and said *I'm not going to hurt you* and how she threw back her head and laughed, the airy loop of it slinging out of her throat and fluttering there, birdlike, before it was lost in a rush of wind. How she looked at him with dark, dark eyes and said *I'm not afraid of you* in a voice that made him feel so ecstatically powerless, it was a fall by itself. *I just don't want you to stop me.*

And yet he had. He had stopped her. He had *saved* her.

The memory of her climbing down from that ledge, so precious to him it was almost erotic.

If only he could remember the truth before it morphed to nightmare, then maybe he could hunt alone. But the truth wasn't what returned. Instead, ghost-Grace looked down from the lip of the bridge and her eyes were golden owl eyes now. Her swirling hair beat dark, muscular wings around her head. And then his mind made her jump. At first it was beautiful, at first she was flying, slow motion, waving her arms, magical again—a miracle! No human body should fly this way! But that moment of recognition bleached the color from the miracle, and suddenly she was only falling, endlessly falling (this vision was always slow motion), and he could feel it too, the forever spin—her body, his body—both of them spinning in circles through the air. White lights, then dark. White lights, then dark. The whirl over and over, a seat belt pressing impossibly hard into his chest, over and over, around and around until finally: stillness. The ticking of some engine, some heart. The rising sound of sirens, but

it wasn't sirens (this took him a while to realize), it was a sound
coming out of his own mouth. He got out of the car. His legs doing
things beyond his control, slipping and sliding on the pavement,
freezing rain in his eyes and something hot in his eyes too, hot and
cold running down together from his forehead. He couldn't stand up,
so he crawled to her body, this magic girl who had flown—he had
seen that miracle, hadn't he, her owl-white parka swooping across his
windshield and into the night—and the sirens in his throat were back
now, and everything was slippery, everything that should be inside
was outside. The unsalted pavement, slick with ice. The sleet on the
girl's broke-open face. Her golden eyes gleaming in the headlights,
unblinking, uncaring. How they wouldn't look at him no matter how
many times he yelled into her face.

The siren of his voice in the dark: *no no no no no*.

The siren of Grace's voice in the dark: *yes yes yes yes yes*.

All of it crushed together, twisting and snarled, whenever he was
alone in the woods.

So—Lana and Hannah joined him. Dulling the shrill memories
with their sweet, downy reactions to hunting: their muffled giggles,
their little-girl chatter, that swimmy way of looking up at him no
matter what he did or said. Everything matted inside him becoming
clean again, washed spotlessly clean by the way they looked at him.
You're good with destruction, Lana had said once, but she hadn't understood that destruction was never the point, destruction was merely
the itch. The point was the scratching—everything rough and bloody
becoming soft again in his hands, stitched whole as it must have been
in the beginning. Like that morning they came upon a herd of six
deer right across the creek—an easy shot, but Peter didn't take it. He
felt stillness in his chest, no urge to start the dying-and-living process
all over again. He pointed across the creek and heard the girls gasp—
deer, they whispered, *deer, Peter, deer!* Like a lullaby, *dear Peter, dear,*

and there was this beautiful split-second calm before the deer flung their heads up in unison, all six springing into one choreographed motion—six mirrored arabesques in a single leap, their fractured and effortless flight over a barbed fence—and then, just as miraculously, gone. Instantly invisible. Only the loud echo of one deer's warning, a throaty keening, lingered behind, calling from a place he couldn't see.

The three of them had stood there together in the dappled light of the woods, the morning that glittered suddenly with wild promise. And as the girls erupted into ecstatic yells—*did you see that, omigod, omigod, did you see that*—he thought how he wouldn't have wanted to see such a thing alone anyway. Not because it was haunted, this moment, but because it was too much beauty for one body to take. Too much pleasure in the emptiness, in having something still out there to find. He didn't notice on this morning, his third-to-last morning on earth, that he was not thinking of a drink, not thinking of Grace, not thinking of flight or a distant horizon. He didn't notice that he was not thinking of anything but this world, living.

VI

Because the stage light behind her eyes had become a strobe. Because the less she slept, the more she couldn't turn it off, a wire increasingly stripped. Because paper skin, paper bodies, and the ripping feeling inside her every time Hannah left for sleepovers at Lana's—earlier and earlier, without a goodbye—the whole house hers to drift around in, smolderingly lonely, for the rest of the evening.

Because late commission work. Because missed calls, missed doses.

Because Hannah, each night, sitting next to his pushed-in chair at dinner: "Hear anything from Dad today?" Her voice so careful and soft, so full of crushable hope, that Grace had to acknowledge her greatest failure, which was not losing her daughter (though that felt imminent) but raising Hannah in her own image. Deferential, too agreeable. No toothy rage to carry her through the distinct possibility that her father was somewhere in pieces right now, that her mother might be next. No fortitude for death, its borderless mystery, the maddening imagining. It made Grace want to do something wild—upend the dinner table, send the dishes flying, shove Hannah hard out the door and into the merciless world, this girl she loved with her whole, messy, shameless heart, because what was love if not a form of survival?

But she just smiled. Her second-greatest failure. "Dad called while you were at Lana's," she said. (A lie: he hadn't called in six days.) "Everything's great. A quiet week on the base. He set some broken bones, fixed a little orphan boy's cataracts. The usual. He says he loves us and he'll be home soon."

Hannah pressed her paper napkin to her mouth and nodded, looking down. Then she got up from the table, slung her backpack over one shoulder, and glanced at Grace before she walked out the door. "Mom," she said quietly, very agreeably. "Cataracts are for old people."

Because the kitchen clock ticking away in the silence. That *tsk tsk,* like a vigilant mother.

So maybe, in the end—Grace wasn't even sure how she felt about this, but the fact was indisputable—because Peter needed her. More and more, in fact, than he had in the beginning. More than Matthew, more than Hannah, the people she loved who (late-night thought, pond-deep thought) might very well be better off without her. The way Peter looked at her now felt like those early, lost years of marriage and motherhood, that sense of being essential to someone, tenuously vital. How urgent his gaze when he made love to her. The way he always kept his eyes open and drank her in, wouldn't stop watching, wouldn't stop making her be *seen*. How tightly he held her, as if she were a lifeline, a route out of danger as they pressed against the walls of the shed, the edges of tables, this tiny space still big enough, but barely, to hold something that she knew was getting larger, sparking at its sharp, flinty edges.

"Don't leave," he told her tonight, afterward. "Don't leave. Stay." His body spent and heavy on hers, face buried in her hair, and after a while the sparks faded to cool reality, as they always did: the plastic tarp they were lying on. The fine skim of sweat and grit that had felt one way a moment ago and now felt the opposite. Electric-blue twilight hummed outside the dirty windows, enough to bring the room into focus, the dead marble eyes staring down at them. Hawk and fox and mouse and bird, the predators mixed up with the prey—she couldn't usually see them there. She usually met Peter in the shed past dark, after she was sure Hannah must be asleep at Lana's, when it was dim enough not to feel the glassy gaze of the animals on her body.

But they were meeting earlier lately, or else the days were getting longer. Either way, a solstice approaching.

"Stay with me," Peter said into her neck, sweetly, needily, and she pushed his body off hers.

"I have a call," she lied, getting up from the floor. She pulled on her sweat pants, her slack tank top. "With a director in San Diego. Tomorrow. I need sleep, and we need to stop."

Grace watched him freeze. A new carefulness in the air. The words had been in her throat for weeks, and suddenly she had released them—hadn't meant to necessarily, but now that they were out, the relief was undeniable. The rush of enacting one's own destruction. The anticipation over. She thought of the drop beneath the Gorge Bridge, of Hannah on the threshold of the kitchen doorway, the black night lapping behind her. At the edges of her mind, strobes flickered.

"We don't need to stop," Peter said quietly. "In fact, we can't stop. You want this as much as me. You *need* this as much as me."

Grace stared at him. His face was smooth and faultless in the blue light. Certain moments he reminded her too much of Matthew, and here was one of them: that earnest gaze, full of vulnerable faith in her. He was so very, very young.

She turned to leave but paused at the door, an animal snagging her attention amid the masses. A mole? A vole? Something larger than a rat, positioned with its mouth wide open, a miniature gun to its head. Teeth tiny and angry as pins. The gray fur was so soft it seemed to glow, and when she reached out to touch it, her fingers tingled with a vivid current—almost alive, she thought. Almost, in a strange way, beautiful. She touched the little black gun and realized it was actually a little black telephone and the darkness pressed harder against her temples. She hated all of them.

Peter's hands touched her shoulders, turned her slowly around.

"This was never supposed to last so long," she said. His eyes were lost in the dark, and she wanted to see them and hate them too, she wanted guts and dirt, she wanted ugly, the dread inside her translated into a pulsing, ugly thing she could name. But he wouldn't stop touching her shoulders with that warm earnestness, and already the hate was cooling, hardening to mere fatigue. She leaned her head into his chest. "I have a husband. You know that."

"You *had* a husband." He cupped her neck, fragile in his hands. Brittle. Mere bone. "He left you. He's insane, but he left you."

"I have a daughter."

"She'll love me. All kids love me."

"You haven't met Hannah. You don't know what she's like."

Peter stiffened against her. Started to say something, then stopped. She tried to push him away, but he held on, he wouldn't let go, and she realized she was crying without sound, and still he wouldn't let her go. He said, "When I found you, you were flattened. You were five minutes from bottom. You *need* me," and something rose inside her like steam, pirouetting white heat. She pressed her face against the smother of his skin. "I saved you," he said, "and you saved me. That's worth figuring the rest out, right? Isn't that worth starting over?"

Behind her, where she couldn't see them, all the rows of glittering eyes, the window and the moon's pale face, girlish and curious. The night electric. The ticking, ticking dusk.

VII

"I don't believe you," Hannah said, and her face was sharp and bright, every angle symmetrical, a perfect face drawn in pen on perfect, clean, white paper. So I told her how I watched her mom take off the tank top—one quick yank over her head—how she threw it on the deer's crooked antlers across the room, how it hung there like laundry. "I don't believe you," she said, and her face was smudged now, but only a little, like crayons but drawn by someone with a lot of control, everything still inside the lines. So I told her how Grace went down to her knees in front of him and took off his pants, how he just stood there, how even the hair on his thighs was gold and he looked like a god, a bronze statue with closed eyes, face tilted up to the moon, while her bobbing tangled head at his waist looked like something he was trying, over and over and over, to press underwater. "I don't believe you," she said, and now her face was one long smear of chalk pastels and the white was blurring into the pink and the red and the fawn-soft brown, somebody's careless hand had smeared itself all over the pretty of her page. So I told her how when he shouted out loud it sounded like the deer when they ran from us, this wonderful-awful moaning, how I could still hear it in my ears in the long silence after, and that's when her face got really ugly.

"He betrayed us," I told her. "We meant nothing to him, can't you see that? We were just a route to your *mom*. Here, have some more," and she didn't argue this time, she just took the can from me and drank, and the foam was filling us up with air, I felt my whole life bubbling hot just beneath my skin. The boys always said beer made you feel hazy, but that was the opposite of what I felt. I felt beautiful in the way the sun must feel beautiful. I felt ready to burst with truth and light if someone could just cut me open.

It was Hannah who thought of going to the shed. Breaking in and tearing apart all those sewn-up little animals, all those bodies we'd salvaged, the dues we'd paid to get this in return. Or maybe it was my idea and I just let it come out of her mouth. We were starting to feel like one person again; it was hard to tell where I stopped and she began, our bodies one body linked by betrayal.

So we waited for my parents to close their door for the night. Zipped pillows into our sleeping bags, popped my bedroom screen, and slipped out into the crickety dark. Our long white T-shirts, matching; our white-and-pink-heart boxers, matching; a second six-pack—my dad's, swiped from the basement fridge—swinging in a Target bag between us. The cracking sound of opening the cans, loud as thick bones snapping. We walked along the shoulder of the empty street and scanned for roadkill, but everything was bare and clean, the pavement, the sky, everything naked with something that felt oddly like joy, everything a beginning. *I love you,* I told her, kept babbling it out because some film had been taken off my mouth and words were pouring free and rich and easy. *Peter doesn't mean anything. Your dad's coming back. Of course he's coming back. I'll help you get through this, you know that. We'll take that fucker down,* and she just nodded. *We'll fix it, don't worry,* and she was done crying now, the snot wiped away, but her eyes were still swollen and raw-meat red, and I loved her even more because of it.

Because why do we treasure the things that are pretty, stitched up and shiny as if it can last? Sometimes love is a wound. A slash in the gut, jagged and wild.

When we got to the shed, the padlock's jaw was already unclamped. I pressed my finger to my lips, though I think Hannah was actually the quiet one, and we shared another beer at the edge for courage. The can, when she handed it to me, tasted sweet like strawberry Chap Stick. Like summertime, like Hannah. Like my dad, after a couple but before too many. I felt the night expanding, including all of us.

Until we walked inside the shed and found them all missing: every shelf bare, every animal vanished. The empty mounts still on the walls, the little props still scattered around—tiny canoes, tiny guns, tiny hats and vests and jackets and buttons—the jars of salt, the stripping tools, the hair dryer hanging from its hooked cord like a noose, the scissors and razors, all of that was there. But every animal was gone.

I felt something breaking open then inside me. Couldn't explain it and can't explain it now—just the sensation of a zipper, a liquid feeling, spilling. I said to Hannah, "I think I'm going to throw up," but I didn't throw up and it kept spilling out anyway. All this light I'd felt inside fading out to the cricket sounds, to Hannah's red eyes, to the dusty outlines left behind by everything that had disappeared.

"Lana? Hannah?"

We heard his voice before we saw him. Turned in the doorway and watched him emerge through the dark, a ghost coming into focus.

"Is that you?"

We waited, Hannah and I. Didn't say anything, but maybe we understood each other in that moment, felt the same blank rage. He stopped when he saw our faces in the moonlight, his eyes stuck in mine. I don't know what he saw there. But sometimes, when I can't sleep, I like to imagine it. I like to think it was something sharp, like the razor on the table, the scissors, the hooks on the walls. Something wild. Something as dangerous as all the things Hannah was suddenly throwing around the tiny shed in a white, winged, swirling rage, angry and loud in a way I'd never seen her, yanking mounts off the walls, dumping salts from the jars, flipping the worktable—all of it flying and blade bright.

But not before he saw it first in me, in *my* face. Not before all that danger was mine.

When the night fell silent, I looked at him, standing there shock-still as a dumb mounted squirrel. Hannah was crying in the doorway, her face turned away from us. I held a razor out in front of me. I don't know how it got there. It was as if it had suddenly appeared in my hand by magic.

I wanted to say to him, *Here. Open me up.*

I wanted to say, *I want you to want me. Not her. Not them.*

Instead, I held the razor higher and said, "Get the fuck out of here." Because that's what best friends do. And when he ran to his truck, eyes glassy and wild, I followed him, but not very far. After a while Hannah came up behind me, her footsteps slow rustles in the grass. I felt her take my hand, the hand without the razor in it, and we stood like that together, breathing the same steady beats, as we watched the headlights fade.

VIII

He's pounding on her front door now, pounding long and loud and watching for her through the tiny window in the door's blank face, long and loud and hard because he knows Hannah isn't home, no one's inside to wake except Grace. Knows he was foolish to think starting over would be easy, but the foolish—he knocks even louder—are still allowed faith. A whole life can be crushed and then saved, a stitch here, some sawdust there, just prop it up and believe in it.

So when he sees her through the window of the front door, walking slowly down the stairs, flicking the exterior light switch as she passes so it floods brightness around him, he is certain he will tell her everything—the girls, the shed, that Hannah must know about the affair, and how protective he feels already toward her, as if she were already his daughter. How important it is that they come clean, tell Hannah the whole truth, ask forgiveness before they embark upon this new life. He is certain Grace will listen, then nod. She will hold him close on the outside steps and say his name. She will open her door and they will float into the house together.

Grace looks at him through the glass of the window, her hand on the knob. Her eyes are feathering at the edges. Her pupils are chasms, that black-hole look he remembers from the gorge.

When she pulls the curtain closed, maybe he shouldn't be surprised. But he is. And when she turns off the light, darkness swooping down around him, something cracks in his chest, an itchy heat that hasn't flared so intensely in years. He feels it still as he pounds on the door, hard, then harder, then lighter, then stops—itch like an unscratched match, rough as the wood against his palms, unyielding. Itch like the scuffed-leather grip of the wheel, the too-fast roads beneath him when he drives away. Asphalt blurs in the headlights' white, abrades itself beneath his tires, but still this blazing itch untouched, this siren stuck in his throat, stuck right in the pulpy dip where his pulse wants out, out, out.

That itch could have lasted all night, flared its way through the darkness, then faded by morning. It would have faded eventually. He could have parked the truck in his parents' driveway, sun just starting to pink the horizon; he could have returned to his childhood bedroom, thought about the endless lonely day to come. The world all around him, spinning. He could have closed his eyes and he could have opened them and a new day could have begun.

Except that it's right then, on that nighttime road, that the white flicker finally returns: pale flash at the periphery of his vision, near the shoulder of the road and coming closer, straight at his truck. White feathers of an owl, white outline of a girl, a cloud on the horizon—it doesn't matter. What matters is the beautiful panic in his heart, the panic he feels once again and the sense that it's right there for the taking, a second chance to grab the wheel and swerve.

He wrenches it to the left, feels the tires leave the ground—

And the joy overtakes him: to feel no impact, to surge forward only through emptiness. Glorious. Flight. He's spinning again and again now, ecstatically back through time, a coil of string winding in reverse, everything coming undone. The stitches are spooling, unthreading the bodies, opening them. The bodies are spilling their sawdust into his hands. His hands aren't taking the guts out, they're stuffing it all back inside, the blood and mess and pulse, stuffing every little thing full of its beginnings, and the skins zip themselves closed invisibly, stitchless, whole again, rise up from his hands—magic.

In Peter's last breath, in the glow of the headlights—which will stay on all night until someone finds him, and which could stay on even longer if they had to, pulsing with gas made eons ago from the bones of some other animal—he catches a glimpse of motion at the edge of the horizon. Peers into the darkness at the lost thing coming toward him. Is it gray fur? Blue feathers? Or the soaring he's hoping for, the torn-open flight of a tiny white body lifting up into space and never coming down?

IX

Months later, after Matthew returns from war, while he sleeps the stone sleep of the dead and the safe, Grace will leave him over and over. She'll drift to the front door, press her face against the glass, and watch the sky, which is never empty—the blind bats darting, the night moths' tango with the porch bulb's deadly gold. Her hand will hover above the trigger of the light switch until she can conjure Peter out there, his face, his desperate hands pounding against the door, and maybe this time will be the last time. Maybe this time, when she cuts the lights, he'll disappear for good.

Because the moths can't help themselves, drawn from darkness to the heat.

Because isn't it a kind of mercy, then? To flick the switch, send them night-bound? To try and save them?

Because her father was a professor of biblical studies, and once he told her the story of the ten virgins.

A gospel parable: ten virgins were waiting together for their bridegroom, who was late returning to them. And yet they were faithful, keeping their watch. Each virgin had a lamp to ward off the dark, but only half had remembered to bring the oil to light it. When the night came, the foolish women with the dry wicks said, Won't you pass along a share of oil, won't you help us fill these empty lamps with light? But the wise women just laughed, understanding their advantage. And when the bridegroom returned, he gathered half the virgins into his arms—only the women who already had what they needed to survive the dark walk—and led them to the marriage feast.

So the foolish virgins stumbled, lampless and lonely, through the woods. Their palms were cut by thorns, faces abraded with scars, knees blackened by dirt they couldn't see to brush away. When they finally found the feast, they pressed their ears against the door, hearing the harsh laughter of the women on the other side. They pounded on the wood and shouted to their bridegroom, Lord, Lord, open up to us, please—Lord, you *know* us. But he came to the threshold and looked out at their bodies disguised by the dark and said, What I will say is true: I am certain I don't know you. I am certain I cannot say who you are.

X

When they found his body, the car wasn't even dented. Still running, not a scratch on it, no evidence whatsoever of the crash that killed him. It was as if the shiny outside of the Chevy had restored itself, come back to life, and Peter was the dead sawdust cost of it.

A heart attack, the doctors guessed, though no one sounded sure.

As for the fire in the shed, they said it came from the salts. Some of them were explosives—lithium and chloride and nitrate and saltpeter—generally used for fireworks, not taxidermy. Turns out he hadn't known so much about what he was doing, and sometimes I wonder what happened to those little animals and their brackish pelts, lined on the inside not with preservatives but with propellants that could have become any color. Just waiting to ignite.

When we watched the shed burn down, we held hands. We thought it might explode into rainbows, each one of those jars bursting with an individual beauty, a brilliant salt for every crayon in the box. But it was just a regular fire. Our T-shirts smelled like smoke for days, and we didn't wash them until our moms made us.

You won't believe me if I tell you we didn't burn it down, so I won't.

But don't tell me I was wrong. To *want* it burning. To want the insides matching the outsides, to want every dust-lined, animal-fled, abandoned space filled with the blazing color it deserved. Don't tell me I was wrong to watch for them returning—I'm still watching for them—those tender, salty bodies, lost and flameless, that were never going to last forever.

That fall they sent Hannah away again. Back to boarding school, where she wrote me letters for a while. She sent me a new Heartthrob card in every envelope, smiling gray faces tucked inside like lockets—Scotty and Bobby and Jake and even Trevor, each a story we had told each other, once upon a time, in the dark. I still have them saved in a box. I don't look at them very often. It's enough to know they're there, that on some cobwebby day I might slice the tape and lift them from the shadows, rift their softened edges across my thumbs, these boys, these beautiful boys, still and flat and waiting, these lives we used to press against our hidden, beating hearts.

There Will Be a Stranger

❧

Dear Mr. Arcilla,

By the time you read this letter, you may be dead. It's possible you have already read it, even as I'm writing it to you. I'm not sure how this works. As a child, I understood death to be a one-way street, no backing up. Like those spikes at the car rental lot, the ones that release their teeth if you drive across them in the right direction and blow your tires if you reverse. NO EXIT, the signs say. SEVERE DAMAGE WILL OCCUR. But I'm older now. Enough to know I know less about death the closer I get to it. Enough to admit it might be less spike than season, less one-way road than roundabout track where the dogs have gone home, but only for the winter.

All of which is to say: it didn't surprise me when you came back.

Though it did surprise me when your car hit mine. Surprise bright enough to empty out every other feeling, even the things

I knew I was supposed to see right before dying. Your whole life flashing before your eyes—isn't that the way it usually goes? Was it like that when you drowned the first time, decades ago? I've pictured death often, and what I picture is thumbing fast through a favorite book, skimming one final, dog-eared time through all the best parts before the lights go out for good. What I never expected was this blank-page feeling, the vacant flash of our fenders meeting on that mountain road in New Hampshire. The calm of it. The slow-motion emptiness. *So this is how it will go,* I had time to think—time, even, to marvel at the plot twist, the irony that my death would happen on this particular day, this particular trip home from the hospital. *So this is how my life will end.* Not with a whimper after all, no moan in the night, no slow cancerous drip, but a beautiful, blitzing bang. I didn't feel afraid. I felt detached and vaguely inspired. I felt the way you feel when you watch a particularly stunning sunset, or the finale of the fireworks display: how beyond your control the whole thing is. How impossible to take it all in, this huge thing that seems to have nothing to do with you, and yet that poetic sense at the edge persists, the feeling that your life has attached itself to a larger beauty. Your car turned the hairpin corner and I saw your tires begin to spit their grip, the gravel fireworking over the mountain edge. I saw the silver smile of your bumper catch the zoomed-in reflection of my windshield—a fun-house glimpse of myself in the curved chrome. You were in my lane. On my right was a mountain, on my left the mountain's drop. Nowhere to go but straight ahead into your fender.

The silver parts kissed. There may have been a spark, though I'm probably adding that now because that's how it felt, like two wires that should have come together long ago. I watched the navy of my husband's Honda dimple and curve, relaxing into the embrace of collision, rolling up in a round wave one would never expect from metal. Opalescent blue glittered in the sun, and just beyond the horizon of it, wide-eyed, familiar—that flash of recognition—I saw your face. You were as young and beautiful as I remembered.

And then the airbag, and then the white. Like any death, I suppose, although I didn't die.

WHEN I WAS YOUNG I had a pet frog. The breed wasn't native to New Hampshire. It was tropical and exotic, bright green with small yellow spots. I had bought it at the pet store, secretly, without my mother's permission, which she never would have given. But it was tedious to make me return the frog once I'd purchased him. I had already carried him home in his little terrarium with neon pink stones and fake ferns for climbing and that plastic toad I'd saved from the dollar store nestled in the back for him to discover later: a friend. And so I got to keep him.

I believed two things at the same time about this frog, two things that couldn't both be true and yet had to be true. I believed he was a prince who could understand everything I told him, all the promises I made: that I loved him and would remain faithful until his transformation occurred; that time would eventually match back up the prince I held in my mind and the frog I held in my hands; that someday we would be together in a different form, our true selves. At the same time, I also believed that the frog was an animal who did not understand me at all, who didn't even know what a *me* was. To his uncomprehending frog eyes, I was a witchy presence on the edge of the plastic universe, regular and inexplicable as the sun, a face in the glass, uninterpretable. And I wanted both of these things to be true. I wanted to be a god, a life-giver that depended on a certain lack of understanding: the beginning of everything. And I also wanted to be the end, the lover on the last page, the reason the life was worth living.

I don't know why I thought of the frog when you knocked on my driver's-side window and woke me up. Your face was bright and shocking in the sudden light, panicky. You were terrified you had killed a woman, and an old woman at that (because I knew you would find me old, because anything over fifty is old at your age). You were horrified at the snaggled maw that had replaced the front of my car, which had spun and crashed into a tree at the edge of the sharp curve, your own car somehow barely dented, though the crash was your fault. Looking back, I can see how unfair the damage was. I can see how that probably made your guilt worse, and how all of it—the panic and guilt and horror—was layered together in the face outside my window. But in that vacant moment when I looked up from the airbag, I had no idea who you could be, or what you could be. Or what I could be, or even what it meant, to *be*.

And then I blinked and I was human again. And you were two things at the same time: the boy who had just totaled the last car I would ever drive, and the ghost of someone I knew long ago. The end, and also the beginning.

YOU WERE A TEACHER ONCE, in the beginning. You were young and shiny and rumpled, and we loved you as only twelve-year-old schoolgirls can love a boy teacher. Puppy love. Isn't that what they say? That's what it felt like, faithfully chasing after you at Briarfield, nipping at your heels, laughing when you scolded us in Spanish because you weren't really scolding us. Anyone could see you loved us too. You made us *dulce de leche* in your free time, the plain white milk turning caramel and sweet. You assigned us Spanish fairy tales to translate and chose the darkest stories from the textbook. I remember the Frog-Woman's twisty golden spells and how she died dancing in the arms of the king. I remember Maria Ceniza, Cinder-Mary, naked in the bath before she turned into a bird. No one had ever asked us to read stories like this before. No one had asked us to put them into our own words, to find ourselves within them.

Las Brujas, you called us. You gave us that gift. That we were not just princesses watching the kingdom unfold but the witches who could change it.

When you drowned in the Briarfield pond, you became our own Spanish fairy tale, just as dark, just as bereft of the happy endings we'd been raised to expect. We all grew up when you died, except for you—our lost love frozen at the bottom of the pond, a boy forever, waiting for someone to lift the curse. As simple as a kiss, sometimes. As commonplace as a meeting on a mountain road.

WE WAITED FOR THE POLICE TO ARRIVE. You had cell service and I didn't. Or perhaps you had a better phone, the next generation. I'm always finding that to be true at my school, which is not Briarfield, but which is a boarding school like it, filled with children who live on smartphone screens much fancier than mine. Boys and girls of bytes and pixels, children of the cloud. I teach literature, and for years I've dragged my students back to earth with the oldest stories, ancient myths and parables—Greek tales of men on long journeys, of women always on the verge of turning into things. But my students still misread them, mistake them for fairy tales. They believe a fairy tale is anything that smacks of magic. They laugh when I tell them that myths are different because someone, somewhere, long ago, believed them to be *true*—a way of explaining the universe. *But who would believe that?* they say. They snap their gum, turn back to their screens to buzz and swipe and click like the strange new species they are. I have suspected for some time, even without the doctors' news, that I should retire early, while the children are still a little bit real.

You offered your phone, told me to call anyone, and I thought of my husband, waiting at home for me to come back from the hospital. He would wonder—not yet, but eventually—where I was, what was taking me so long. I told you no, that I had no one to call.

But a doctor, you said. Your head—please, someone. You were terribly concerned about the blood on my face, the gash where my forehead had hit the steering wheel. I knew it was just a scratch—I would confirm this later—and bleeding heavily only because that is the way of head wounds. (I can tell you now that it has healed nicely.)

No doctors, I told you. I used my teacher voice, an ironic way to speak to you. But it did the trick. You stopped arguing, and then I could really pay attention to the weird thing: the way you were glowing, there on the side of the road. Not so much light that I noticed right away. Just a little sparkle at the edges, as if the pixels of your body were taking some time to crisp up. Another boy of the cloud. Up close, your features were more familiar than they should have been considering I hadn't seen you in decades. Your forehead was tan and unwrinkled, heartbreakingly smooth. You had freckles. Of course you would have freckles.

You helped me out of the car, cleared me a seat on a log in the shade of the maple tree that had stopped me before I went over the edge. The tree's branches were thick wristed, wide and flushed with July's unapologetic green, almost eager. *Old friend,* it seemed to be saying to me, *you have returned at last,* and I looked away, couldn't meet its gaze.

We listened for the sirens, but there was only the small talk of nature—vague crackle of the forest, the hum of the river below the mountainside. It seemed awkward not to acknowledge that you were a ghost, just as it would have been awkward to acknowledge it. I used to feel the same way looking up at the end of dinner and seeing a bit of toilet paper on my husband's cheek from the morning's shave. To say nothing felt cruel. But to say something would be to admit we hadn't looked at each other all day. My husband has a beard now, but these awkward-nesses never go away. They just evolve. You learn to coexist with them. You realize one day that the new truth living invisibly between you is nothing more than the old truth in a different form. A polite silence about bodily vanity—the toilet paper, the new mouth wrinkles, the taut stomach loosening with age— becomes polite silence about something interior, deeper and just as unspeakable. My husband hasn't really wanted sex in years, for instance. To say this out loud would be to excise a wound that has healed nicely on its own, that has not been a loss so much as a tacit adjustment. We make our careful way around the topic. We make space for it in the bed. The truth sleeps between us, like a baby, a vulnerable thing we have been put in charge of by the universe. This does not change the nature of our love, only the shape of it.

And so I'm wary of speaking that which doesn't need to be spoken. This was advice you gave me yourself when I stumbled over Spanish words that wouldn't materialize in my mind. Take your time, you told me then, pointing to the list of verbs. You don't really need the vocabulary yet. That will follow. All we care about right now are the forms, the conjugations. Once you have the forms, you can fill the shapes with any words you know.

Now, on the mountain, you sat your cloud body next to mine. You told me your name was Henry. I nodded, though the name felt wrong and strange, didn't fit the shape I had saved for you in my mind. I don't believe I'll ever think of you as anything but Mr. Arcilla. Our best teachers are like that, their influences frozen into a certain identity that a first name, however perfect or unfamiliar, can never truly change.

YOU WERE GOING TO A WEDDING, you told me. Down the mountain, at a little country club I knew but had never been to myself. Friends of yours from the college you'd graduated from just a month ago, a point of fact that made me sad: you would drown in the Briarfield pond at twenty-two, in autumn. You had only months left. I tried not to dwell on it.

They'll get fireworks tonight, you said. I didn't know what you meant. The bride and groom, you said. Fireworks, on the wedding night, right? You blushed, as if embarrassed at the talk of sex, and I remembered my own wedding night, many years ago now. How it felt less like fireworks, that cheap dazzle, and more like the sea—calm, smooth, then rocking, then building and crashing like tides that would move in and out for the rest of our lives. A miraculous thing, to hold the one you love on your wedding night and know that it has arrived—the rest of your life—as huge, as fathomless and invisibly bounded, as ocean. Much more interesting than fireworks.

But then I realized what you meant. It was Independence Day. There would be fireworks of the literal kind. What a lovely day for a wedding, I said. What a lovely holiday, though I didn't really believe it. Fireworks struck me as garish for a wedding, like a too-big diamond. They say it will be clear tonight, you said, and I nodded because yes, I had heard the same.

THE ROAD AT OUR FEET was a mountain road, but not a normal New Hampshire mountain road. New Hampshire is a granite state, its foundation hard and bright as silver. A schoolgirl friend who would grow up to be a climate scientist—Nellie, of course you must remember Nellie—once taught me about the rocks of New Hampshire. She told me that an earthquake here would be more destructive than the same earthquake in the soft-bellied soil of any other region. Like a struck bell, she said. The vibrations would clang and linger, resound against the granite, shake our architectures to the ground.

But the road at our feet was silky and reddish, like clay. It looked almost sweet. I remembered the strange cravings I had once, before the doctor diagnosed me with gestational pica. How I wanted, at certain times during pregnancy, to eat clay, only clay. It became a fixation, almost sexual, like a secret but essential fantasy I kept in my head while my body did the mechanical part. At dinner I might be chewing what I was supposed to be chewing, the thick gristle of red meat, the kale's cellulose green, the prenatal vitamins. But what I kept in my mind was the clay. Its smell like peaty scotch, the dirt and stink of fine cheese. An oozy clamp between my teeth, sticking.

You drew pictures in the clay while we waited. There had been a storm last week, and the ground was still loose enough to hold the deep outlines of what you drew. A cow, a barn, a pail of milk. A happy sun in the sky, a bell with a zigzag crack. The Liberty Bell, you said. Happy Fourth. You handed me the stick, and I stuck it hard into the road. I twirled it until what I had drawn was a small, black hole. Shards of clay heaped up on the sides like the piled dirt of a dog burying a bone. This took a long time, and you watched me patiently. Still, there were no sirens, there was nothing but the dapple of sun on the ground and the titters of birds we couldn't see. I pinched a little woman out of the piled-up clay. The Frog-Woman, I said, thinking you'd remember the translations, the Spanish fairy tales. But if you did, you made no indication.

The clay stuck under my fingernails. The woman was formless and lumpy, an inarticulate shape that looked more like a man. I placed it next to the barn and the cow, and you added fireworks above it all in arched, dotted lines. They burst up and outward like half-bloomed flowers, stretched their tips toward the middle of the road. At some point a car would flatten them, but for a moment they stayed like that, half opening, ceaselessly opening—even now I can see them there, opening—in the storybook we'd drawn together.

I took your hand. I pressed our hands together, tightly, and held them against my legs. You looked awkward, thinking the gesture was more than what it was. It wasn't that. It was just that I could feel myself losing the grip of something I'd remembered for a moment: what it's like to stand at the left-hand edge of your life and skim ahead, the feeling that there are so many more pages to go and it will always be like this. There will be a stranger, whom you know and do not know, to look on with you, a sound in the trees that you keep thinking is a siren when it turns out, again and again, to be the looping call of an invisible bird.

WHAT I WONDER, as I write this, is what I hope to accomplish with it. You have already brought me home. We have already said goodbye. I have watched your dented car drive away around the bend with the knowledge that I will almost certainly never see you again in this life. Not because I think it's impossible to return, but because both of our days are numbered.

And yet even as I write these words: there is your car again. There is the bend, returning.

When my son died, the milk came in anyway. It felt like the most cruel joke nature could ever play on me. Not the least because it hurt. My breasts had been tender and raw for months, but now they hardened like stones. I cried in my sleep if I accidentally rolled onto them. Eventually they leaked, milk that was clear and yellowish, that looked tainted. I kept it all inside me, wouldn't release it even though I craved the release like I craved the taste of dirt. And eventually my body sucked it all back up. In the last days there was just a tiny pocket of soreness beneath my left arm, a single swollen duct. A little factory whose diligent workers didn't know it was time to quit, that the market for milk had collapsed. I pressed on it every day, kneading it like clay, a satisfying pressure that brought with it a sweet little lick of pain. Until one day I reached for it and it was gone, dissolved into the rest of my body.

When the lump returned several years ago, when I found it inside my breast with my fingers, I let myself pretend. Just for a second. Time folded into itself like a letter, a perfect crease down the middle. I could feel my life mirroring backward. I knew this lump was the end. But what it felt like was the beginning. It felt like everything else would follow in reverse: the last lick of milk, then the stony tenderness of holding the milk in, and the tiny baby in my hands, froglike, too small to breathe. Then the belly like a little globe beneath my shirt, and the clutch of my husband against me, inside me, his breath in my ear, our loud laughter in the tangled sheets. It was the most delicious lie, and I savored it until it was entirely gone. Perhaps this is why I'm writing you this letter: to remind myself, and you, of the things we can't return to, which are so easily disguised as the things we can. To remember that death might be a racetrack, around and around, but time is the teeth in the parking lot, that love is the borrowed car.

IN THE DISTANCE there were swimmers on the far edge of the river, hardly visible. I could see them clearest if I didn't look straight at them: a woman, a man, another man, a dog. They might have been teenagers; I couldn't tell from where we were. If it were fall, I would have been worried they were students from my boarding school, breaking the rules to swim in the river, which has faster currents than children are used to and granite rocks sharp enough to slice their silver deep. But it was July. The students were scattered, gone for the summer, safe at home in their invisible homes.

I watched the dog jump in, get out, jump in again. He was brown and mottled like the river, the fur matted and clumped. But when he shook himself off in the sun, the droplets of water made a yellow corona around his fur like a halo. Sometimes it followed him into the water, as if his ugly dog body were actually a golden ball sunk deep beneath the surface. I could still see him glowing underwater, even from up here on the clay road, though this may have been a trick of the light, just the sun breaking into its pixels on the river. Or a trick of my eyes, perhaps: that strange, bright sensation inside them. The same thing used to happen after chemo, all the edges of things hazy, as if I'd looked too long into a bright room and now my eyes had to adjust again. A video of the world slower to load than the actual world.

You were anxious. The police were taking their time, and your phone had died. Perhaps the police were not coming. You wanted to bring me to the hospital, to get down the mountain, to see your friends get married before it was too late. But I'd had enough of hospitals, and you thought perhaps you would get in trouble if you left the scene, even to take me to the doctors against my will. Your body was glowing brighter now too, a current lit up with its own anxiety. You kept asking me to say something, to distract you while we waited for help to arrive. Say what? I asked. Anything, you said. Tell me about your life, tell me a story, any story you know, a dream, a fairy tale, just keep talking to me, don't go to sleep, please.

The swimmers dove in. They climbed out. I thought about telling you the story of your own death in the Briarfield pond. How afterward we used to cry for you at the edge of the water and cast hopeful incantations, even pray to you, as if you were an invisible god who might hear us. I thought about telling you how good it felt to make up stories about you, search out explanations, rewrite your history so we could fit inside it—who was with you the night you died, who had loved you, kissed you, lain down with you—lies that were so delicious, they began to seem real. Each myth a way to bring you back to life.

But I was wary of saying any of this out loud. At best, I

thought the idea would be lost in translation; at worst, I thought it might be rude. (How does a speaker politely describe the listener's impending death?) So instead I told you the story of the frog prince. A princess lost her golden ball in the pond and a frog promised to retrieve it, but only if she would marry him. Inside his frog's body he carried the spirit of a handsome prince, the man he would become. But the princess didn't believe him. So she lied to the frog, broke her promise, threw his little body against the wall when he came to her bed. Somehow this became a happy marriage, in the end. I knew I was missing some steps.

Still, you nodded. Your face was encouraging. I remembered this same look during oral exams in Spanish, a look like if you nodded enough, if you bolstered us up with your eyes and made us believe the words were there in our mouths, they would suddenly appear beneath our tongues like magic pills, unswallowed and whole.

Keep going, you said.

So I told you about the Frog-Woman. She was never in disguise, never a pretty thing hidden in a frog's body. She was always mottled and ruined and warty, always a frog, unapologetically honest about who she really was. And everyone fell in love with her anyway—the prince, the king, the women of the village. They brought her to the castle and the Frog-Woman danced what turned out to be her last dance, spinning, laughing, throwing bones into the air and turning them into gold. It was a beautiful dance, so beautiful that the other women tried to copy her. But their bones were just bones, and eventually someone hit the Frog-Woman in the head and she died.

That's a funky myth, you said.

It's not a myth, I said. It's a fairy tale.

What's the difference?

Myths are about why things are. Fairy tales are about how they could be.

But aren't they basically the same, in the end?

I said, They're not the same. My mouth was sandy. I said maybe that was enough storytelling for now. The swimmers dove into the water, over and over, and we watched them. The sun glittered off their cold, shiny bodies. They clung to each other on the shore for warmth. But in the water they loosened their orbit and drifted, fought the tug of invisible currents alone. How strange, you said, that a single fairy tale could have such different endings. I don't think you understood that I was telling more than one story, that each ending would depend on its beginning.

THE FAIRY TALE I DIDN'T TELL YOU is that I have crashed into that tree before.

It's a knife-blade turn. It sneaks up on you if you aren't familiar. I've seen the ghosts of other cars through the years, the snaky aftermath traces of skids. After a rain, temporary waterfalls short-cut down the road to the river, so the muddy ground is often saturated, ready to fossilize the evidence of miscalculations: the brakes that chatter their antilock jaws, the back tires that swerve before straightening. At certain points in spring, when the wet days veer suddenly into dry, careening heat, the deepest gashes will scab for months.

What I'm saying is, this is the sort of place where memory stamps itself hard. Which is why I recognized the tree immediately. The tree is where I met my husband.

I was younger then. Older than you, old enough to believe I was the grown-up I would be for the rest of my life. When in fact I was still so young. I had just turned twenty-six. I was living at home in New Hampshire after many years away, going to a community college that I liked well enough but that my mother, who'd invested a small fortune in boarding schools, thought of as her personal failure. My days were spent avoiding her harping corrections and laments, of which there were many; twenty-six years is plenty of time to gash up your own road. Nights, I'd sneak out my bedroom window and drive to Boston or the quarry and press myself up against the sharpest edges I could find, exhilarating brinks, the gasp of a high ridge, the gritty after-hours of smoky nightclubs. I could see by then that I'd somehow folded my life into the wrong order: a childhood far from home, an adulthood trapped there. What I wanted was to feel on the verge of something. I wanted the right-hand edge of whoever I'd become, because surely this wasn't it.

Sometimes I went running along this mountain road before my afternoon classes. That's what I was doing the morning I met my husband. The road, with its tight blind turns, wasn't an especially safe route for running. No shoulder, let alone a sidewalk. And the hairpin curve by the old maple was an even worse place to stop and stretch; those mud tracks, many of which came right up to the tree, were a danger sign I could read just fine.

By the time I looked up, it was too late. My husband's tires were already singing, the gravel a silver spray. I couldn't see the driver for the sunshine on the windshield, a white screen getting brighter and larger, as if to swallow me with glare. And then the screen snapped into focus: the pond-blue length of the car as it lost control, began its sideways spin, that long, sleek body a deadly glisten in the sun. My feet were snarled in the tree's clenched roots. My muscles were frozen with shock so immense, it bordered on calm. I closed my eyes and waited for the end, hoped it wouldn't hurt.

But it wasn't the end. The car stopped short, inches from my belly. I opened my eyes, and the man who got out was sheet white and speechless. He was older than I was—a full decade, I would find out later—and in that moment I could see the ripples of smile wrinkles around his eyes, the moonlight glint of silver at his temples. He stared at me, the trunk of his car between us, and we both pressed our hands against the warm metal, and I had a feeling then, the same feeling that is the shape of a word on your tongue, a recognition of meaning before you remember the word. What I felt in that moment was something like *woodsman*. Or *huntsman*. Any of the strong, coarse fairy-tale men. I thought of burly arms, large, practical hands, fatherly and effectual and a little bit brutal, and none of what I imagined in that moment would turn out to be true—my husband is the type who calls me from another room to kill a spider, who leans in to smell the newspaper ink with deep, simple appreciation before reading. But standing there, intact, unscathed, the story I imagined was the one I wanted, the one that could carry me forward out of my life. And so I chose to believe it.

Just as he wanted to believe the story he told me later: a white-haired princess had leaned out of a tree, sucked his car right up to her belly, caught it with her bare hands, and made him fall in love with her. He would always tell the story this way. It became a thing, a bookend to my own fiction. He told it to his coworkers at the school where he maintained the grounds, his colleagues who would eventually become my own colleagues. He told it to his mother and to mine. Whenever he told it, he would pull me close and I would feel the smooth press of his lips against my cheek and the story would thrill me the way it has always thrilled me. He believed I was the princess, not the witch. And I let him believe this. Despite the dark histories I carried, and the dark futures too—the little knots that hadn't yet formed, the broken promises, the unbroken curses—I could give him this gift: the belief that the woman he saw beside his car, the princess he had already fallen in love with, was me.

What a story, he would say to our smiling friends. What a story we'll have to tell our children one day. And I would nod, I would say it back to him in the dark, laughing, and we would pull each other close, we would say it until we didn't have to say it anymore because the story was already here, the ending had arrived, inexplicable and oddly shaped, there was no more future tense, and the story was our life.

WHEN WE HEARD THE FIRST EXPLOSION, you jumped up. I'm not sure what you thought: that it was a gunshot, maybe, or another car crash. Or perhaps the smashed Honda, which had been breathing steam from its punched-up mouth the whole time we'd been sitting there, had finally surrendered to smoke and the whole thing was about to blow.

It took some time for us to recognize that the sound was coming from the swimmers. Firecrackers, the shrill kind I don't like, all shock and no dazzle. I felt my headache clamp tighter on my temples, turned toward you to complain. But then I saw your face. This glow, this little-boy excitement, as you looked down at the swimmers and their firecracker games—how lit up you were once you realized the sounds weren't gunshots or back-fires, that they were merely the sounds of joy. I think I caught a glimpse then of the child you used to be, a child who must have loved firecrackers, and probably dogs and rivers too, this younger version of you that was still there, hiding behind the slipping mask of adulthood. For a while I'd been trying hard to stay focused, but now I was fully focused. Your face had shaken me out of the ache in my head and into a different memory.

What I remembered then was the chapel at Briarfield—the service they held after you drowned. I remember the chaplain saying that only now, in the darkness of your death, were you able to stay young forever. It was our collective duty, our *responsibility* (she could wield this word with tremendous gravity), to ensure your immortality by remembering you as the bright young man you'd been. In our memories, she said, you would never grow old, never suffer the taunts and aches of aging—the embarrassments of the body, its tectonic collapses, the broken hearts and losses the rest of us had coming, and the hearts we would break ourselves, the fractures we would not only suffer but cause. Instead, you would live on as a young man inside us: golden, joyous, without worry or care.

Of course we recognized the chaplain's lie for what it was, a way to gussy up your death. Still, she made death sound like the better deal. I sat there in the hard pew, in my girl body already mantled with pressure, and added this new load: my need to keep you alive. A witchy power that carried none of the *brujas* magic, that carried only burden. Remember, remember, remember. To forget would be to kill you all over again. Every night, for years, I made myself picture you before sleep, running breezily through the dapples of the campus towpath, wild and shirtless for the rest of time, grazing your fingers along the tall grasses of my mind.

I think something's wrong, you said, leaning forward.

For a moment, I thought you meant something was wrong

with my memory. Things were, in fact, getting a little blurry. I'll confess—even now, as I'm writing this letter, I'm not certain it was the chaplain who said all that about joy and care and duty. It was so many years ago. It might have been the headmistress. Or the doctor, or the stillbirth counselor. Or my husband. Even there on the mountain, sitting in the shadow of the tree that nearly wrecked me twice, I felt a split-second moment of unease, a kind of queasy double vision—the sudden sense that I wasn't sure who you were anymore, this stranger sitting next to me.

And then you were racing to the edge of the mountain, pointing at the river. The swimmers below had gone frantic and wild. They were waving their arms. There were only two of them now, running back and forth along the shore, and the dog was barking somewhere with bright, clanging barks that rang hard against my ears. The third swimmer surfaced briefly in the river, then went back under. He's drowning! you shouted. Oh God! Oh God! He's drowning! You were searching for a gap in the guardrail, a grassy trail that would lead you down the steep embankment. Already, you had taken off your pullover.

When you died the first time, you were naked in the pond. I remembered that as your shirt came off, the fact of your long-ago naked body. That shocked me once, schoolgirl that I was. Back then, naked meant only sex and secrecy, the carnal wants of the living body that we kept under careful wrapping. But now, watching you shed your clothes, it seemed the most logical form for death. I knew, if you entered that water, that you would be lost to me, that I would have failed the chaplain's directive. I knew your body would return to the place it had come from, enter the river the way frogs enter into hibernation in a pond—heart stopped, breath stopped, waiting for the seasons to change, for the cycle to restart itself—and that you would drift along once more to a place I couldn't see, naked as the day you were born.

And then you paused. Just before you flung your leg over the guardrail. You looked down at the third swimmer, who was whooping and splashing now with the dog in the water, holding something up in the air—a ball, or a bone. A spent firecracker, or something unexploded and ruined now with water, a thing dragged off the silty bottom, thrown and retrieved. We couldn't see it clearly in his hand. But we could see that the people on the riverbank were laughing. They're fine, you said, sounding almost disappointed, and you put your shirt back on and came to sit beside me on the log. Your hands were shaking. I didn't reach out to hold them this time. They're fine, you kept saying, they're fine. You started to cry. You cried in a way I had never imagined you crying—a gut-splitting cry, a little-boy sob that mixed you all up in my brain again, a cry that was its own awful, beautiful, unexpected sound. I put my hand on your back, just lightly, just a little, and you didn't pull away, but you didn't stop crying either. That came only a long time later, after the swimmers had quieted and the bright barks of the dog had dimmed, once the only sound was the river running its course. My hand still and light against your shirt.

I suppose this was a happy ending. Two happy endings, two near-deaths-but-not, on the same day, in the same place on the mountain. It didn't feel like it, though. Is that really why I'm writing you this letter, to tell you I was disappointed too? I keep picturing what it would have been like to watch you jump the guardrail at the road's edge. Your body would have flickered with sunshine as it ran through the dapples between the trees, half glint, half cool shade, until you reached the riverbank. Maybe I would have felt something tug loose—a freeing feeling—the tethers snapping in my mind, that long cord finally cut. Or maybe I would have felt nothing at all. Who's to say what it's like when we finally let go? You might have jumped to the bone-cold bottom and dragged your fingers through the silt, the water witchy with seaweed, the dark impenetrable. You might have felt your hands close around the invisible man, then brought him back to the surface, gray, unbreathing. You could have held him close. You could have pressed your hands over and over against the water-full lungs, the one-way doors of his heart, believing in the promise of any body, which is that inside this machine of muscle and bone is a luminous life, golden and carefully built, and all we have to do is throw ourselves hard enough against it. For the door to open and the eyes to look up, blinking, startled, and know you. For the hands to let go. For breath.

BY TWILIGHT, I asked you to take me home. I was feeling better. The ringing in my ears had stopped. My body felt dazzled now, lighter than it had felt in months, and no, I did not need to go to the hospital, thank you very much, my home was just a few miles away. I knew your name, I reminded you. I would call the police tomorrow and explain. And so you nodded. I think you were relieved, if you want to know the awkward truth, if you don't mind my acknowledging it.

I will tell you now that I did call the police, just like I promised. But I didn't tell them you were there with me on the mountain road. I described the accident: how I had lost control all by myself and nearly driven off the edge, the consequence of misdirected attention. I ordered a tow and my husband cried and they all believed me. It was an easy lie, a tricky curve; anyone could take it too fast. It's simpler this way, you see, and I hope you will not object. I hope you will understand that this is not a gift for you but a gift for me. To know you have been unburdened, these last few months, from the human entanglements that would have followed—the insurance filings, the police statements and court dates. This is the gift I wanted for myself, to imagine your final days in this life untethered.

By now, your college friends are married. I thought of them often in that first week after the accident. I liked to picture them in a tropical place, at the edge of the earth in a landscape filled with long, flat beaches and impossible blue water. Of course, they must be home by now. But I let them stay there in my mind far longer than I should have, each day pretending that today might be their last day away, that they were looking at a storybook sunset together, enjoying the view before their real lives began. For a long time, I saved them there.

When the truth is, I never knew them anyway. Wherever they were, wherever they are right now, that is their real life. Separate from me and rolling on by itself without my having to keep them alive with my mind.

YOU DROVE ME HOME in your dented truck. My house was so close, we could have walked. I hadn't told you that before; I had told myself the information was inessential. But of course telling you would have meant explaining the direction I was driving, which was not toward home but away. It would have meant acknowledging that I had already been home once that day, that I'd returned from the hospital and idled in the driveway, my husband inside the house, waiting for news but not expecting bad news. The tests were supposed to be routine. I was in remission. This was the story that still existed in my husband's mind, that could not coexist with the story I was going to tell him.

And so I had driven away. Just minutes before I met you. I wouldn't have gone far, I don't think, probably not much farther than the tree where we crashed, or perhaps the end of the mountain road I used to run on when I was young. Maybe I would have stopped at that long, delicious stretch at the finish—the crest at the bottom of the mountain, the fire in my lungs, the way even with my muscles shaking from fatigue, my body shutting down in protest, that last downhill pass would always feel so easy, as if I had no body at all. Not far, then. Just far enough to let that other self, the old me, the one still living in my husband's head, keep living a little longer.

You asked me, as we drove, if I wanted to confess something. A strange question, though it felt natural enough at the time. I suppose I could have told you this story, my story of driving away. But I said I wasn't sure what you meant. So you asked if you could confess something to me. Of course, I said. Anything. And you told me that you wished it were true: that the man had been drowning in the river. Outside the window beside you, the sky was purple with almost-night. The trees were empty silhouettes, and you drove so slowly that they didn't even blur, each one its own clear shadow. You glanced at me to see if I was shocked, which I wasn't. But to humor you, and because you seemed to want to say more, I asked why.

Because I wanted to save him, you said.

Why?

Because I almost killed you today, and I thought maybe that would undo it. That maybe I would be even. I would be back where I started.

But the man is alive, I said. Isn't that the same, in the end?

You said, It's not the same.

The street lamps were blinking on, one by one, as we drove beneath them. I thought about going back to where I started. I thought about my husband's face at the tree, as white as a ghost, as hard as a huntsman, and my mother's hands, callused but gentle, helping to smooth the soil where we buried my tropical frog when he died. I thought about how he'd looked in my little-girl hands at the pet store, as webbed and tender and promise packed as any life, and the way you always rubbed your own hair absently in class, twirled your cowlick between your fingers, a quirk you've probably had since childhood. I thought of the way our bodies contain their beginnings—all their ghosts, all the habits and contradictions that make us human, and how tenuous they are, these loosely architectured selves, and how essential. It was meaningless to go back to where I started. I could feel that we were already there. I could see, looking at you in the violet light, the teacher I used to love. But I could also see the little boy who twirled his hair to go to sleep at night. And I could see the man who would cry with me at the side of the road above the river, who would let me comfort him as we looked down at death, looked it square in its ugly-dog face, and said no. And I could see all the rest of you too—the gap-toothed boy, the grime on the knees, the brave hands that would clench a bike's rubber grips, that would sing with the metal of a baseball bat in spring. The boy who would read storybooks with a tented flashlight, who would lean in to smell the newsprint like he saw the grown-ups do, who would get lost sometimes in the sunset above the outfield. Who would listen when his mother was calling, and know it was time to come in from the dark.

You gave me your phone number and address, your full name and insurance information. You wrote it all down on a piece of paper, and I folded the note into a deep pocket when you drove away. It's still there, in the hall closet, in the summer coat I probably won't wear again; the days are cooler now, the nights brassy and sharp with the chime of fall. But I held it between my fingers as I stood on the porch, watching your taillights blink away through the trees, watching the night come down, the milky stars that dripped from elsewhere. I wonder what my husband will think if he finds your name, months or years from now, in the pocket of the coat where I will leave it. A meaningless name, the penciled outline of anyone's life, a call he could make, or not, to a stranger. Sometimes I picture him there, on one end of the phone line, reaching out invisibly into the cloud and waiting for you to answer.

But not then. Then, I opened the door and I took off my coat and I went inside to my life. Where my husband had stayed awake for me. Where he would say to you, if he knew this story: thank you for bringing me home.

Yours,

Lilith

In the Hollow

———— ❧ ————

O F COURSE, HE KNEW she would return to him. Thirty-seven years they were together before she died, thirty-seven years of days and nights, of fingers tangling in the dark, of unspoken agreements. Thirty-seven years of pith-bitter arguments and resolutions sweeter for the pith. Thirty-seven years of children imagined, distantly on the horizon, and of children nearing, and of children receding before arrival. Thirty-seven years of a quiet house. Thirty-seven years of the knots in her hair and the way only he had the patience to undo them; and later the knots in her shoulders and the way only he had the strength to press them out; and later the knots in her breasts and the way he finally, ultimately, couldn't. And even then, thirty-seven years of the way she moved, the lyrical sway of it, down the sidewalk, down the aisle, through the twisting hallways of his mind, with him or not, bedridden or not—still, even then, the way she moved him. He remembers how she would slip one strap down over her shoulder at a time, first the right one, then the left one, and how it never failed to drive him crazy, even at the end, even after thirty-seven years.

So—he knew she would return to him. He just didn't realize she would come back as a tree, and even now, sometimes, he finds himself forgetting. In the kitchen, cleaning fish or stirring a brandy, the tinkle of ice in the glass like a light clearing of her throat, and there she is, an invisible presence behind the closed door of the study, or a far-off rustling in the kitchen. He'll spend whole afternoons believing she's in the other room before he looks up from his newspaper, smiling a little, ready to call out to her, to tell her this strange new thing he's read about—and he remembers.

That's when he'll go to the window, or out to the back porch where he can see her best, and apologize. "I'm sorry, Lilith. I forget sometimes." She never minds. At least he doesn't think she minds. It's harder to see her in the daytime beneath the wood and the leaves, harder to hear what she has to say, and at night he always forgets to ask. It's usually at night when she undresses and comes to him, her hands smoothing the bark off her shoulders, first the right one, then the left one, that slow-motion slippage still catching in his chest every time. And when she emerges through the rustle of branches, pulling leaves from her hair, luminous, breathless, walking toward him in the moonlight, he doesn't usually remember much of what he was thinking during the day.

He has to admit, it sort of makes sense that she would be a tree. There was the initial surprise, of course, and maybe there was even a tinge of disappointment (because why not a dog, a cat, a houseplant—something that at least lived inside, that he could care for a little better?). But in the end he knows it was the right choice. He can tell when he watches her from the kitchen window, sees how happy she is—the birds in her hair, the sun all jittery in her foliage, the great vibrant rustle of her life now, and it makes him feel lighter, knowing what she must be feeling. It's like watching her stick her head out the passenger window of their Honda, the way she used to whoop and close her eyes against the wind, sun in her face, hair all ablaze with the day. Or when the breeze in the backyard picks up and runs its fingers through her branches, everything rippling to one side and her long, bare neck exposed—the luxurious stretch of it, her chin tilting back, waiting for him to run his fingers along the hidden, tender part of her jaw.

Even in her darker moments—the deepest heat of summer, leaves drooping, branches slack, the whole world humid with memory—he knows that exact space in that exact shade in that exact corner of the backyard is exactly where she wants to be. Home inside herself, tapping a private history he can't access, a series of tunnels beneath her fissured surface—veins drilled by insects and birds and secrets, interior maze humming with the sweetness of sap and the darker molds of rot, all of it invisible to him. On days like that, he leaves her alone to be with her thoughts. And when he sees her later in the evening, stepping out from beneath the privacy of her own shadow, he can always tell something has calmed within her, settled, a thought rooting back to its proper place. He holds her face in his hands then, tells her, "You know I would do anything to make you happy." And she nods, her eyes shining with sun.

So—yes. A tree. It makes as much sense as anything.

THEIR LITTLE HOUSE, the house of thirty-seven years, is at the top of a small hill in southern New Hampshire. In the back the land opens up to lush, muscular curves and grassy planes, spans of urgent, wild green he once spent long weekends taming, but the front porch overlooks a neighborhood. At the bottom, nestled in the crook of a dark valley, is a little boarding school where he works as a groundskeeper and his wife once taught literature. Early in their marriage, they would sit on their porch and listen to the voices rise up from the valley, the shouts and laughter of invisible, parentless students blurring together into a beautiful silence, an empty hum he never noticed at the time because its promise was always there. They would talk, with vague and obvious assurance, about the future. Sometimes they would squint through the glittering leaves of the trees below and guess at who they were, these distant, anonymous children moving through the hollow: the bookworm, the athlete, the romantic, the one who got away. They did that often, and then after many years they did not, and he remembers her saying once as she looked down at the children from the edge of the deck, "It's funny how they never change. Year after year. They're always just the same age."

That's how time feels to him now, especially in daylight. Like a held breath, a dreamy vertigo, that feeling of moving forward when he knows, deep down, he isn't going anywhere. He can no longer hear the children from that same spot at the prow of the deck. He has tried to catch a glimpse, but new structures have been built and he doesn't recognize the view.

SOMETIMES HE CAN'T WAIT FOR NIGHT, and when it starts to feel that way, a hitching-ticking feeling in his chest, he goes to put his hands against her and wait. That feeling of the bark beneath his skin. Empty dips and grooves, the furrows and creases he can lace his fingers inside—they remind him of the mysterious teenage scars up and down her arms, a razor-cut record of stories she never really told him. He imagines someday-lovers, long after he is gone, knifing initials into her tree-bark skin, a line of deep gashes, and he wants to cry because it gets mixed up in his head, it feels somehow like the future has already happened, time bending in a way that eclipses him. He presses his fingers against the wooden gnarls kinked along her trunk and tries to find her. The slim shoulders underneath his hands, the impossible knots, furls of ache too dense to disperse.

He'll wait there until he is holding her again, until the only feeling in his body is the deep, still certainty of hers.

It astonishes him sometimes, how much he never noticed the life of a tree before. These creatures breathing all around us, motionless, immortal, or so close to it they might as well be. So constant and unchanging, we take them for granted. She is warm in the sunlight, rough and quivering between his palms. He presses against her and closes his eyes, and he can feel the world sway, he is sure she is moving against him. *Did you feel that? Right there? Right there. Try again.* And he does. Waiting, as still as he can make himself, her breath rising and falling beneath his hands.

THERE ARE TIMES when he's not sure what's appropriate. For instance, he'd like to tie a swing to her, the type he had as a little boy. Nothing fancy, just a wooden plank, a few ropes from the garage, a place for him to sit when he visits because he gets tired from standing and he's afraid to sit on the ground at her feet. "My knees, my back," he tells her. "Old bones. They don't rise up so easily anymore," and they both know that's not really it, but neither admits it. That's one of the things he loves about her: the way she still knows what not to say.

But he's not sure he should do it, if that sort of thing is allowed. Rope seems like something you should ask about first, and it never feels like the right time to bring it up, especially in the moment. (How had they asked for things once, in bed? He recognizes only now that there was touch and desire and understanding, but never language, never a trading of their darkest, most secret wants.) So he just stands there, even when his legs get shaky, and he gets a little annoyed with her then—although he knows it's not her fault, that he's the one who hasn't figured out how to say what he is thinking. He tries not to let it show, and when she asks him what's wrong, he tells her he's only worried about the weather.

Because that's something that makes it hard: the weather, seasons, storms and frosts and ice and time. She tells him not to worry, that she's built for this. But he doesn't think it will ever be easy for him to watch nature roll in, that great uncontrollable beast, fickle and shameless, ready to shake his wife to pieces at its whim. In the winter especially, it's hard not to notice when her body grows stiff, contorted. She tries to hide it when they're together, but when she stands there alone, looking out at something invisible to him, he can tell there's an ache he won't be able to rub away. He watches her face, stark against the harsh white landscape, and it's the face she had at the very end. But something about it reminds him too of an earlier part of their marriage—the first baby they lost, the second one, the expression she wore when he asked if they could try again. A wintry look, lonely, as she turned toward him to answer. *You know I would do anything to make you happy.* Turned toward him, but she was looking at some-thing else, something he couldn't see from his part of the world.

HE DOESN'T KNOW how long she's been a tree when he realizes she's starting to change.

It's subtle at first: a glint in her brown eyes that he hasn't seen in years. The way it's hard to keep up with her when they go for walks in the moonlight—never far, never the threat of not making it home before daylight, just far enough to pretend that they could keep walking. She breaks out one night with this laugh that reminds him of why he first fell in love with her—this sheer, brazen joy, a sharpness of being that had smoothed itself through the years into a patina of marriage and age and tempered expectations, a polished chuckle. But here it is again, that first laugh—bright, jagged burst that preceded everything—and it's then that he realizes: she's getting younger.

Once he notices, he can't stop noticing. The sunlight in her branches first thing in the morning, flushed and dewy and crazy with shine. The buds bursting open with a springtime exuberance they never had before. She shakes her head and the world frays with light, birds sailing out of her long hair—blond again, a flyaway gold full of highlights and warm-toned shadows.

"Slowpoke," she gibes on their evening walks. "Hurry up," and he wishes he could, wishes more than anything he could hurry up and forget.

BUT HE'S CHANGING TOO. Hands a little shaky on the morning coffee cup. The way everything has started to smell the same, taste the same. A flutter in his legs. They're quiet at first, these subtle betrayals of his body, but moving toward the observable, the dramatic. He slips once in the kitchen, on an invisible slick of spilled dishwater, and it takes him ten minutes to get up, and even then he can do it only because he's dragged himself over to a chair. It occurs to him suddenly that when he jokes with her about his knees, his back, his old stubborn bones, he's actually telling her the truth. That's when he gets scared. He has no idea, for a moment, what other lies he's telling her that might be true.

"We'd like to see you again next month," says the doctor in Boston, smoothing a bandage over the cotton ball on his arm. "For more tests." The doctor is a tall, slim woman his wife's age, red hair grayed in a way that reminds him of November: silvery branches, the last crimson leaves cleaved against the coming winter. Her finger-tips on the most tender, interior part of his elbow feel as delicious as betrayal. When she notices the tears in his eyes, she misunderstands and presses her hand tighter against his skin. "I'm sure it's nothing to worry about," she says. "Just a follow-up." She has hazel eyes that remind him of cut grass, that sliced-clean smell, a truth he will never tell his wife.

In the meantime she is growing more and more, or less and less, young. She is tipping backward into the woman she used to be, and there's something beautiful about it, and there's also something lonely. The deep, grooved furrows of her skin are smoothing out to seamlessness, and he doesn't know where to place his fingers anymore. The loose rustle of her body is snapping taut again, and there are times he thinks he should look away from her nakedness, not sure if it's right to be with this woman who was once his wife but hasn't been for a long time. She has the firmness now of their middle years together, the strong arms, the steady gaze, a solidness that startles and shames him. An impatience too that defined a certain period of their lives, and he remembers now her need to move quickly from one activity to another, to never stop, to endlessly *do*. She takes up hobbies at night—gardening, star charting, the things she used to love before her hands and eyes betrayed her—and sometimes, when he's watching her in the moonlight, kneeling down before a plot of stubborn begonias or tracking a constellation he can't see, her lips (full again) pressed tight with pleasurable focus, he thinks it might not make a difference to her, right then, in that moment, if he weren't there at all.

SOMETIMES, STORMS. They used to worry him, even when they were first married: the rogue *what-if* of lightning and a surge of wind, the threat of a tree falling onto the house. And of course it got worse once she died. He remembers how he used to go outside with two umbrellas and stand beneath her dripping branches as if he could do something. He stopped when she asked him to, reminded him that standing beneath her in the middle of a storm was not the safest place to be, and secretly he was relieved. He didn't think anything in the world could feel more helpless than waiting there at the foot of that tree, holding a closed umbrella, wishing with all his might that he could help her and knowing that he couldn't.

Now he doesn't worry about her so much. Now she seems to know what she's doing. There's even a part of him that wishes, perversely, that something might happen during one of these storms: a sudden flash and the rocking weight of her timbering into him, the house exploding with bright broken glass and leafy darkness—warm, wet, rushing, then silent, their bodies tangled, the sweet destruction of going down together.

ONE NIGHT HE TRIES to talk to her about it. They are planting asparagus, pressing dark soil over the new roots—a little too hard, he thinks. No way those delicate shoots will break through with the dirt packed down so tight. She says, "It won't produce for three years, you know. It needs time to build a strong root system." She smiles at him, an impish smile. "This is a long-term investment in asparagus. I sure hope you aren't thinking of selling the house."

Her eyes are bright. Her skin is so clear, so radiant, it breaks his heart. She can't be more than twenty. "Lilith," he says, and he hears the tremor in his voice, and he realizes the shaking is already there in his jaw, his hands—how quickly that comes over him these days. "I don't know if we have three years."

What he means is that she doesn't have three years. He can see that already, knows it's coming, her backward life slipping by so fast that he feels he's missed whole stages of her adulthood. What happened to the year she chopped off all her hair and hated it? Or the time she got bronchitis for three months straight and couldn't speak, could use only a rudimentary sign language, learned to joke with him in signs, invented whole phrases of inappropriateness with her hands? What happened to her thirties, to the babies? It's as if she's skipped certain parts that she doesn't want to remember. Long spans of their marriage conspicuously absent, whole losses lost.

She doesn't answer. She only shakes her head when he starts to speak again, looks up sharply when he keeps trying. She blinks her long lashes at him and tilts her head, brushes a hair out of her eyes with the back of her dirty hand, and he's transported suddenly to the base of her tree, the memory of this same pleading look: *Just stop talking.* The way she turned away from him, glanced down at her hands, covered with dirt, and paused for a moment, as if she couldn't remember where it had come from. Then she pressed her fingers back into the ground, smoothing the newly turned soil, packing it down a little too hard.

That was the first time. They hadn't known what to do with it—too small to bring it to the doctor, to even call it a baby, but too large to ignore the fact of it, the need to *put* it somewhere—and so they'd buried it in a corner of the backyard, beneath the shade of an old cottonwood. He'd always wondered if that had been a mistake, to bury a secret so close to the house, and he wondered again when it happened the second time. After that they decided not to try anymore, and they rarely went into that corner of the yard—almost never in the rest of their thirty-seven years together—until she became a tree.

"It takes a certain kind of patience," she tells him now, looking down at the ground and the buried asparagus plants that won't ever, in his mind, give them asparagus. "To wait that long for something. A kind of faith. Nothing visible in the soil, no way to know for sure there's anything in there. No way to track it except by memory." She looks up at him, and for a moment she isn't twenty, she's as old as she ever was, and she knows everything that happened, everything that's going to happen—all the ghosts inside her waiting to take shape, all the new growths and cells dividing, the future becoming itself by becoming smaller.

Then she smiles at him and takes his hand. "Let's just try to forget," she says. She pulls him up and starts walking through the yard toward the house. "Forget we ever planted asparagus at all," and he's having trouble keeping up with her, can't see her face as she moves farther away from him. "We'll forget it to find it again. Think of the surprise a few years from now. Think of how wonderful it will be, when it all comes back to us."

HERE IS THE PART that comes back to him:

There was a time when he dreamt every night of a baby. A bright red squall, slippery and terrifying, just born. Thrashing limbs, violently beautiful with blood and urgency and aliveness, unquestionably kicking. In his dream, every time, she handed him the baby and her face was young and glowing, cracked open with joy. But the tiny body was too slippery to hold, and every night he dropped the baby on the floor. Woke up with a throat so tight he thought he was dying himself, woke just before the little body hit the ground, and all day he would find himself waiting for that crack, the impact he knew was coming, would never be strong enough or quick enough or father enough to stop.

He never told her about the dream. And what comes back to him now is not the dream itself but the way it felt to keep the dream a secret. To hold a vigil for the loss that was wholly his own invention, a horror he would never let her near enough to touch. That private ghost buried deep in his body. It made his world feel somehow (unfairly, deliciously, impossibly—would he ever understand this?) closer to hers.

SOMETIMES HE FORGETS that their circumstance is unique, that other trees don't feel the same things she does. He'll catch himself walking through town, nodding politely at the blank-faced saplings planted along the sidewalk, only to feel a lurch when they ignore him. Or an ache of sympathy when he drives to Boston and sees a newly paved parking lot along the way—gutted horizon where there used to be clusters of pines. Popsicles have become complicated, every bite on the wooden stick like snapping at someone's finger, and maybe there's something playful in that, even a little indecent, but it's never long before he remembers. That this stick is just a stick. That no branch is an open hand. That the hungry yowl of razed sky, no matter how empathetic it feels, is nothing but an emptiness, as indifferent to him as it ever was.

Which is why sometimes he lets himself forget on purpose. And suddenly a walk through the woods is a kind of reunion. The elms bend over the oaks to say hello. The crumpled faces of ancient sumacs seem to understand him, and the elated shimmers of aspen leaves are as frantic as the hands of children, waving. At the end of the block, an untended scrub brush, that scrappy gang of neighborhood boys, rustles and chuckles and plots some new adventure. And anywhere, everywhere, the sigh of the willows will move him to tears.

He times his walks so they end at dusk, when the pond in the woods holds the golden light loosely. Along the far shore a copse of thin-wristed birches glows white. Slender as teenage girls, they gather at the edge of the pond and lean together conspiratorially. They turn their pale faces away from his. If he catches the eye of his wife among them, it's only briefly before she disappears behind the curtain of her unkempt leaves, the tangled limbs of the other birches. But he can hear, even from this distance, the titter of something whispered across their highest branches. He can see dark shapes winging from limb to limb, life laying claim to the gaps.

"Any other symptoms?" says the red-haired doctor each month. "Besides the dreams, I mean." And when he tells her he feels moss growing on his north side, or the deep-ear itch of a squirrel's nest, she laughs. Her leaf-green eyes go dappled and bright. Her human voice is a warm rain in summer, a hum the whole drive home, wet shine fogging off the pavement until it's gone.

THERE COMES A TIME when he realizes she's too young to kiss. She wears her hair in two braids now, white blond and tangled, comes to him with scabbed knees and missing teeth and huge dark eyes, and he realizes he has never known her at this age—hasn't known her, in fact, for quite some time. Yet she looks exactly as he knew she would, bursts out of that tree and into the night with the same jagged enthusiasm he remembers, and he falls in love with her, in a different way, again and again.

The blood test comes back clean. So clean it's a bright, bleached taste in the back of his throat.

They still go for walks together. They dig up earthworms and point out the flowers. Late one night they drill two holes in a high, thick branch, bolt a swing, and he pushes her back and forth in the moonlight while she tells him she wants to know it all—about the world, about their life together—and in her jabbery excitement he hears, he remembers, how it felt to be at the beginning of everything.

HE FOUND HER out there by the tree only once during their whole marriage. Perhaps she went there more often, but he doubts it; she was good at finding ways to distract herself. But it happened one night that he couldn't sleep—woke himself from a dream and realized she wasn't next to him—and when he walked to the kitchen, he could see her through the window at the edge of the yard. Just standing there, her back to him, looking up at the stars through the still-bare branches.

"I didn't mean to wake you," she said as he walked across the cold grass. He stopped a few feet short. There was something in her voice that suggested she wanted to be alone, and he waited for a moment, watching her. The way her pale hair, braided down her back, seemed to glow in the darkness. The way her shoulders still had that thrust to them, that solidness, an ability to bear. This was before she got sick for the final time, but only just before, and he wonders now if maybe she could sense something he couldn't—a tangle gathering, a cancerous root slipping down into the crevices of her body, somewhere deep enough that no one would ever unearth it.

"You didn't wake me," he said. "I was dreaming."

"About what?"

"People." He put his hand against her shoulder. She felt as steady and immovable as ever, fixed fast to the ground. He could lean against her and she would never topple, and he loved her for this, and it crushed him. "I don't remember what else it was about," he said.

She looked at him and tilted her head. She'd been crying. He could tell. Then she laughed her quiet, smoothed-over stone of a laugh, as devastating as it was calm: a rock dropped into water, everything shattering circles outward but her. A laugh that was broken and happy and sad and with him and not with him, a laugh that was only her own, and in that fractured second he caught a glimpse, far beneath her solid surface, of a current running fast and invisible and away from the place they were standing.

"That's always the way with dreams," she said. "People too. Gone before we know what they mean. I'll bet we won't remember this tomorrow, either. Will we?"

"I don't know," he said, and she kept looking at him, and she took his hand. He nodded. "Probably not," he said, and then she led him back to their bedroom, where they slept curled against each other until late in the day.

IT HAPPENS, IN THE END, just as he knew it would: the nighttime comes, and when she doesn't step out from beneath her branches, when she doesn't answer his call, he moves toward the darkness of the tree and finds her there, waiting. A little baby in the grass, too young to know him, too young even to smile. He picks her up and holds her, and there are a thousand things to say, and there are no words for any of them. The puffy eyes squinting up at him. The deep, pink furrows of her newborn skin. The tiny knot of her mouth tightening and loosening, rooting in the dark, and the face that is both hers and not hers.

He sits down on the grass. He knows that soon the sun will come up, that the day will open its empty eye and blink, light sliding across the sky and all the shadows sucked back into the things that made them. But not yet. Right now he just holds her, rocking. It's not a betrayal of his body this time, the rocking back and forth, and it surprises him a little to realize that. How steady his hands are in the middle of this moment. How firm his jaw, how still his legs, how sure he is of his ability to hold her and rock her until the night is over. He tells her, "You know I would do anything to make you happy," and she curls her little fist around his finger.

Below him, the ecstatic tickle of grass against his skin. Above him, the shush of the rustling leaves. Somewhere in the distance, the breeze picking up, murmurs traveling from branch to branch, then falling still, the night holding its breath, and the way he's holding his breath too, everything quivering with the hush of it. She stretches her arms and the trees throw up their hands, the whole sky full of them, reaching through the dark.

Acknowledgments

⟡

Thank you, first and foremost, to the poets and translators whose myths about women inspired these stories, and to the teachers and colleagues who introduced me to them. I owe particular debts of quotation or paraphrase to the following texts: The passage that Lilith reads aloud in "The Translator's Daughter" is excerpted from Stanley Lombardo's translation of the Salmacis and Hermaphroditus myth in Ovid's *Metamorphoses*. The concept of the eidolon in "Helen in Texarkana" is adapted from H.D.'s book-length poem *Helen in Egypt*, itself an adaptation of Stesichorus's *Palinode*. The parable of the virgins in "Ten Kinds of Salt" is adapted from the New International Version of Matthew, chapter 25. And the recounting of Cinder-Mary and the Frog-Woman in "There Will Be a Stranger" is adapted from J. Alden Mason's article "Four Mexican-Spanish Fairy-Tales from Azqueltán, Jalisco," originally published in the *Journal of American Folklore*. I am deeply grateful for the work of these authors.

Thank you to the editors of the following journals, in which some of these stories originally appeared: *Black Warrior Review* ("The

Translator's Daughter"), *Memorious* ("Helen in Texarkana"), and *Shenandoah* ("Ten Kinds of Salt"). And a special thanks to Beth Staples for her wonderful edits.

Thank you to my extraordinary agent, Alex Glass—for bringing this collection to the world and, well before that, for sticking with me down the long and meandering road of writing it. You recognized in its earliest drafts what it could become and set me off, again and again, in the right direction. What's here in these pages was built on your steadfast guidance and insight.

Thank you to my incredible editor, Kate Nintzel, whose every suggestion was charged with wit and warmth and brilliance. You helped me find the structure of this book, and for that, I am so appreciative. But I'm forever in your debt for the influence you had on these characters, whom I didn't truly know until your edits helped me see them clearly. Thanks also to the team at William Morrow and Custom House, especially Molly Gendell, Vedika Khanna, Suzanne Mitchell, Mumtaz Mustafa, Dale Rohrbaugh, Eliza Rosenberry, Ryan Shepherd, and Margaret Wimberger: your collectively amazing work made this book a better book, and me a better writer. I am so lucky to get to work with you all.

Thank you to the institutions that supported me as I worked on this book. To the MacDowell Colony, the Ucross Foundation, the Corporation of Yaddo, the Virginia Center for the Creative Arts, the Vermont Studio Center, and the Sewanee Writers' Conference— magical worlds, each and every one—thank you for the precious gifts of time and community. I'm particularly grateful to the Bread Loaf School of English, another magical world and the place these characters were born, and to Phillips Academy, for the support, the sabbaticals, and the best colleagues ever.

Thank you to my writing teachers for their lasting influence. I am so fortunate to spend my days splitting time between two jobs that I love, and your collective example is the reason I can. Thanks especially to Greg Ulrich, Stephen Schwandt, Edmund White, and Joyce Carol Oates, for the earliest and most important lessons; to Dan Blanton, for introducing me to the many versions of Helen of Troy; to David Huddle, whose course was the spark of this book; and to Christine Schutt and Tim O'Brien, for helping me shape the final pieces.

Thank you to my earliest readers, every one of them brilliant and essential. To Clare Beams, Amber Caron, April Darcy, Kate Ellison, Mike Harvkey, Paul Hurteau, Ariana Kelly, Bill Lychack, Stacy Mattingly, Keija Parssinen, Randy Peffer, Lewis Robinson, Paul Russell, Anne Valente, and Laura van den Berg, thank you for offering these stories, at the various stages you encountered them, exactly what they needed at that moment to move forward. Special thanks to Annie Hartnett, for helping me recognize the bird's-eye shape when I was lost in the weeds, and to Johanna Lane, for the edits, faith, and friendship that got me to the finish line.

Thank you to my many families. To my parents, Jim and Linda Benson, and to all my Minnesota family and friends: your love and support are the bedrock beneath me. To my McQuade family: thank you for accepting me as one of your own. To my Princeton family, near and scattered: you make me the luckiest. And to my Andover family: Thank you for being my village. There is no community I'd rather call home.

Huge heartfuls of thanks to Owen, Ella, and Bridget—my magic-makers, my writing-camp cheerleaders, my persistent reminders that all bedtime stories must include adequate narrative conflict. ("Pwoblems, Mommy, don't forget the pwoblems.") I love you. Thank you for teaching me wonder.

And to Jimmy—truest of partners; keeper of faith in this book, and in me, when I had none left; builder of the fairy tale that is our life. Thank you, wholeheartedly and impossibly, for everything. This is for you.

About the author

2 Meet Kate McQuade

3 A Conversation with Kate McQuade

About the book

9 Dangerous Women: An Essay

14 Reading Group Guide

Insights,
Interviews
& More . . .

Meet Kate McQuade

Sarah Jordan McCaffery

KATE MCQUADE is the author of the
novel *Two Harbors*. Her fiction and
poetry have appeared in *Black Warrior
Review*, *Harvard Review*, *Shenandoah*,
and *Verse Daily*, and her nonfiction
has appeared in *The Lily* for *Washington
Post*, LitHub, and *Time* magazine.
She is the recipient of fellowships and
scholarships from the MacDowell
Colony, the Sewanee Writers'
Conference, the Women's International
Study Center, and Yaddo. Born and
raised in Minnesota, she teaches at
Phillips Academy in Andover,
Massachusetts, where she lives on
campus with her family. ❧

A Conversation with Kate McQuade

Q: *Several of these stories were published previously as standalone stories. When did you start to envision them as part of a collection?*

A: In my mind, the stories were linked almost from the beginning. The only true standalone was the first story I wrote, "In the Hollow." I wrote "The Translator's Daughter" just a few weeks later, and as soon as I did, I could sense some kind of book-length project connecting the two of them. Every subsequent story was my attempt to figure out what that book was. At one point, the manuscript leaned toward a novel, with Lilith taking on a central role; at another point, it was a much looser collection linked only by theme, not character. The manuscript had to try on a lot of different shapes before it found one that fit.

The key turning point in that search came when I drafted the motherhood stories—especially "Wedge of Swans," "Helen in Texarkana," and "Ten Kinds of Salt." The more I worked on them, the more they seemed to be echoing the stories I was telling about teenagers. I realized what interested me most were these parallel times in women's lives when we're on the cusp of metamorphosis—identity shifts and bodily changes so transformational they can feel surreal, even magical. The book's final form arrived when I decided to assemble those transformational stages chronologically—adolescence, motherhood/not-motherhood, death—and to give the Seven Sisters one story each, one metamorphosis at a time, so that they could collectively assemble the full arc of a woman's life across the book. ▶

A Conversation with Kate McQuade *(continued)*

Q: Your first book, Two Harbors, *was a novel. What drew you to the short story form?*

A: I love stories because writing them feels more like solving a complex, meticulous puzzle than writing novels does. Your job, as a story writer, is to evoke a whole world in the same way a novelist must evoke a whole world. But a novelist has more space to wander, more time to linger on those world-building details. A story writer must be much more efficient at establishing resonance between plot and theme, character and setting, style and subtext. Your details have to work harder for you. That's why I think the story's closest relative is probably the poem, not the novel. You don't have time to hit single notes in a story, any more than you do in a poem; you have to seek out chords from the beginning.

I also think a story's brevity deepens the sense of mystery that draws us to storytelling in the first place. I often quote Joy Williams to my writing students, and in her wise words, "the work of the writer is to keep the story from becoming what it is about." My stories always start with some superficial mystery, something that I know from the beginning will drive the plot: Mr. Arcilla is dead, but we don't know what happened. This weird stuff is coming out of a woman's skin, but we don't know why. The crows have descended upon the house: what do they mean? The work of the story isn't to answer those mysteries—that would be to let the story "become what it is about"—but rather to explore why those mysteries matter to the characters. That underlying, character-driven mystery is where I find any narrative's real energy. And I think the compression of the short story concentrates it more than novels do.

Q: Myths and legends come up throughout the book. Why did you work these ancient narratives into present-day settings?

A: I suppose, in the context of this book about translators, the myths were my way of occupying a translator's role. Most of us are pretty good at recognizing sexism that limits women in ancient, classical texts. We aren't always as good at recognizing limitations placed on contemporary women, despite the spotlight that recent cultural dialogues—#MeToo, Lean In, and the like—have cast on questions of female empowerment. In *Tell Me Who We Were*, I was playing around with myths not because I was interested in rewriting the ancient stories, but because I wanted to shine a different light—hopefully a clarifying light—on what it looks like for women to be limited *today*. I wanted to translate some of the frustrations I felt as a girl, and that I've felt as a woman, through the forms of these older stories.

From a process perspective, the myths also helped me move forward by giving me a craft rule to follow—a "thing" that each story would do. I love writing with structural constraints (I prefer writing form poetry to free verse, for example) because constraints are like little fences in my brain; they prevent my writing from slipping into the same well-worn grooves I'd usually glide along if the fences didn't prevent me from taking them. The structural rule I set for myself with this book—that each story would reference an ancient myth about a problematic woman—made the actual writing more interesting because the rule guided me to landscapes I wouldn't have otherwise found. ▶

A Conversation with Kate McQuade *(continued)*

Q: How much research went into this book? What was the most interesting thing you learned?

A: A lot of my early research focused on the myths. But I tried not to take that research too far because I didn't want the book to become overly allegorical. I wanted my characters to feel real, like contemporary women you might know, and I worried that overemphasizing the myths might threaten that familiarity. So in each case, "research" meant learning just enough to establish a conversation between the ancient myth and the contemporary story, and no more than that. The rest of my research went into learning about my characters' professions and passions. Work matters a lot to me, and I want it to matter to my characters. But I need to understand their work in order to write about it authentically. Conveniently, my favorite form of writer procrastination is to throw myself down weird internet rabbit holes. I spent a lot of time learning about ornithology and cicada life cycles and the blog life of amateur taxidermists. I lost more hours than I care to admit looking up smartly dressed squirrels on eBay.

Q: You've talked before about being drawn to "strangeness" and "weirdness" in your fiction. What do you define as strange or weird, and why is it important to your work?

A: I think my fascination with the weird is really just a fascination with humans, especially bodies and the way our identities are shaped by those bodies. For most of the seven years that I worked on this book, I was either pregnant or nursing. My body was in a constant state of dramatic change. And that was nothing compared to watching my children transform from helpless little snuggle-balls into fully formed people with all the requisite fingers and toes, plus surprisingly divergent opinions and personalities. What could be more fascinating than people?

How can literature ever live up to how wondrous and weird the human body is, this constantly changing container that houses who we are? I'm drawn to stories that can make the familiar strange, and the strange familiar, because those kinds of stories remind me to pay attention to how magical everyday life is, particularly the people around me.

Q: How much of this book's setting is inspired by Phillips Academy in Andover, Massachusetts, where you work?

A: I should clarify immediately that Briarfield is not Andover. I am happy to report that my place of employment is less traumatizing, and better at student oversight and support, than Briarfield ends up being for these girls! That said, I'm interested in the way that boarding schools—indeed, many academic institutions—offer a blank slate to students who come from far-flung places. I didn't go to a boarding school myself. But I do remember what it was like to be a middle-class Midwesterner taking that first step onto my college campus (East Coast, ivy-covered) and feeling both welcomed into another world and totally fraudulent. I remember realizing there were whole tiers of privilege above me I hadn't been aware of, a lack of awareness I tried to hide—my first experience with imposter syndrome, I guess. At the same time, being an imposter offered a tantalizing anonymity: not a single person on that college campus knew who I was. I could reinvent my identity if I wanted to—from the quiet kid to the popular one, from the nerd to the party girl—and no one would be the wiser. I could become anyone I wanted to be.

The entire time I worked on this book, I was living in a freshman dorm at Andover. (Running a dorm was part of my job for many years.) Every September, I would watch girls new to the school navigate similar questions of identity. I would marvel at how incredible they were, to manage those questions ▶

at a much younger age than I did. And I would be reminded, again and again, of how simultaneously terrifying and revelatory that blank slate felt. All of which is to say: Briarfield isn't Andover specifically. It's more of a stand-in for institutions that destabilize our sense of who we are, sometimes for the better, and sometimes for the worse.

That said, I definitely stole much of Briarfield's landscape, including Mr. Arcilla's ill-fated pond, from my dorm backyard.

Q: Which authors inspire you?

A: Toni Morrison, who was the master of everything, but who inspires me most for the way her stories can exist on two planes simultaneously—the supernatural and also the historical, the magical and also the real. Anne Carson, who is so good at making the mythical feel modern. Alice Munro, who gives me permission to be wild with time. Tim O'Brien, who writes about memory better than anyone; likewise, his writing about writing. Sylvia Plath, who reminds me that the personal can be political. And so many contemporary fabulist writers—Helen Oyeyemi and Karen Russell in particular—for teaching me to recognize what the rules are by breaking them. ❧

Dangerous Women: An Essay

Tell Me Who We Were began with this photograph, Wynn Bullock's *Woman's Hands, 1956,* which I first encountered in the summer of 2011. For weeks, I kept coming back to the image, knowing I wanted to write about it but not quite knowing how. Something about the way the hands pull at the bark reminded me of a woman undressing—peeling apart the tree as if it were her own shirt, about to be shed—and the wonderful strangeness of that idea stuck with me. I wanted that strangeness to be at the center of a story, even though the draft felt out of character as it arrived, breaking rules I hadn't realized I'd internalized until I broke them. ▶

I'd always been a realist writer, but the story that came to me was unapologetic about its magic. I'd always thought of nature as mere landscape, a passive backdrop to the action; but in my story, as in the photograph, nature exhibited something closer to character. Perhaps most surprisingly—and most satisfyingly— the woman who took shape as I began to write was an older woman I wasn't accustomed to seeing in literature, or in culture. The sensuality of her hands, parting that fissured bark with an almost sexual intimacy, seemed wonderfully noncompliant with societal norms, an undoing of myths we still tell about elderly women, which is that they have aged past desire and desirability. I imagined that the owner of those hands took pleasure in breaking the rules. Even when the story was finished, I wanted to learn more about her.

I don't remember thinking consciously about the symbolism of trees as I wrote the first draft of what would become "In the Hollow." The magic of the tree was, from the beginning, simply a fact of the story, a truth about this woman who also happened to be a tree. (One gift of writing from a photograph is that the world is already made for you, freeing you to consider not why things are, but what results from them.) That said, I must have recognized on some subconscious level that by writing about a woman inside a tree, I was tapping into a long mythic lineage. Greek mythology, in particular, is a veritable forest of women: Daphne, who hides from lusty Apollo by transforming into a laurel tree; Pitys, whose scorned lover changes her into a pine in fury; Philyra, so mortified after bearing her rapist's monstrous baby that she becomes a linden in shame. And the Greeks weren't alone in turning their women into trees. Countless other cultures include similar myths, a reflection, perhaps, that what we historically expect of trees we also expect of women: steadfast immobility and passive silence, an ideal backdrop for the stories of men.

The tree myth that guided me down the path to this book

was the myth of Lilith, Adam's first wife. In Jewish mythology, Lilith asks Adam to be her sexual equal rather than her superior. He refuses and she leaves the Garden, exiling herself to a faraway land where she lives alone inside a tree, cursed with the task of killing her own newborns. She is, in short, a rule-breaker, someone who does womanhood "wrong." She refuses to submit to male desires: wrong sexually. She craves gender equality: wrong socially. She kills babies rather than nurturing them: wrong maternally. Her tree becomes both container for and concealer of her bad behavior.

As ancient as it was, Lilith's story felt familiar. Over the seven years I spent working on this book, I had three children in quick succession. Between births, writing sprints, falling hopelessly in love with my kids, and long periods of time during which I believed I'd never write again, I spent a lot of mental energy critiquing my own bad behavior—partly my lack of writing productivity, but mostly my imperfect motherhood. Being a woman of childbearing age in America means constantly pushing against the confines of a particularly limiting and pervasive myth, one that boils down to: *You're doing womanhood wrong, no matter what you do.* You're wrong, first and foremost, if you don't have children, because women my age are expected not only to have children, but to want them and to explain their absence if they don't exist. At the same time, you're wrong if you do have children, wrongness by a thousand cuts: You're wrong to go back to work; you're wrong not to go back to work. You're wrong to try attachment parenting (suffocation); you're wrong to try cry-it-out (emotional distance). You're wrong to skip the meeting or the deadline, but don't think about guiltlessly skipping the dance recital. You're wrong to leave your kids for ten whole days to go to a residency to write a book about all this wrongness (because the day care teacher: "Why so long? They'll miss you so much!"). And you're wrong to leave your ▶

Dangerous Women: An Essay *(continued)*

kids for only ten days to go to a residency to write a book about all this wrongness (because the residency administrator: "Why so short? Is it even worth the trip?").

You're wrong to worry all the time, lest you become overbearing/controlling/hysterical/high-maintenance— but also trust your instincts, because mother knows best; why didn't you speak up when you recognized that something was wrong?

Granted, I had been practicing my whole life for this inescapable wrongness. Haven't many of us? As girls, we're taught to be pretty, but not dangerously so; humble, but not invisibly plain; confident, but never bossy. Shorten your skirt, but not so much. Raise your voice, but not so loud. #MeToo, but did you really? Shoulder the judgments of tiny deviances long enough and you won't even notice it anymore, how easy it is to tamp down who you are, let alone who you want to be— to bury those possible selves beneath the steadfast, fissured, hopelessly immobile, and deeply rooted expectations of others.

To call a woman's desire for full humanity "bad behavior" is, perhaps, the oldest story, one we've heard so many times we know it by heart, or don't really hear it anymore. I decided to tell it again in this book. I wanted my stories to be about contemporary women behaving badly—girls who break rules, mothers who resist self-sacrifice, would-be childbearers without children—only this time, I'd tell their side of the story. I also wanted to trace the ancestry of that bad behavior, to give my modern myths about women the bones of their ancient counterparts. Lilith's narrative helped me reframe "In the Hollow" around her myth, and that inclusion led me backwards to the rest of the book, and to the other mythic women who provided the framework for *Tell Me Who We Were*. Eve, Helen, Andromeda, Salmacis, the Sirens, countless others: to be honest, myths about dangerous women weren't hard to find. It turns out that a lot of our most lasting myths are about how the fall of mankind results from a woman's refusal to stay uncurious, undesirous, invisible—wrong.

I tried to give those rule-breakers new life in these stories, to let them have the odyssey instead of the steadfast silence. Late in *Tell Me Who We Were*, Lilith explains that the difference between myths and fairy tales is that myths were once believed. Myths, she says, explain why things are; fairy tales imagine how they could be. Although the origin of this book is rooted in mythology, a root I trace back to my first encounter with Wynn Bullock's bark-parting hands, I hope the final result might be less myth—less immobile, deterministic past—than a fairy tale's open possibility. What if we reimagined female desire not as deviance, but as the stuff of common humanity? What if we took the myths we keep telling about women, deeply rooted in our literature and lives, and shed them layer by layer, book by book? Who might we be underneath? ᕬ

Reading Group Guide

1. How does the short story form impact the narrative? Why is it well-suited for the overarching story McQuade is telling?

2. The short stories are set in the present day yet intimately tied to classic myths. What do the myths add to the stories? How is McQuade manipulating literary tropes?

3. In what ways are language conventions broken in the stories? How does McQuade's style add to your reading experience?

4. In "The Translator's Daughter," Mr. Arcilla is described as the girls' "first real love, our first real loss." How does that compare with the love the girls felt for Lilith?

5. How do the girls deal with the trauma of Mr. Arcilla's death and Lilith's departure? How do those early experiences play out differently in their lives as they grow older?

6. "A Myth of Satellites" is told in the second person. Why do you think McQuade wrote in this style? The other stories in *Tell Me Who We Were* are told from a variety of perspectives. How did the shifting points of view affect your involvement in each story?

7. Birds appear in many of the stories. What might they signify? What other motifs does McQuade use?

8. McQuade writes that "In the Hollow," which focuses on Lilith, is the story around which the rest of the collection is built. Why is Lilith such an important character? How does her myth inspire others?

9. Which was your favorite story? Why? ∾